The Lost Dogs of Shoretown

A
Koko the Canine Detective
Mystery

By Annie Mack

Copyright © 2005 by Annie Mack

ISBN 0-7414-2857-1

Cover photos by Paulette Frankl.

Published by:

1094 New DeHaven Street, Suite 100
West Conshohocken, PA 19428-2713
Info@buybooksontheweb.com
www.buybooksontheweb.com
Toll-free (877) BUY BOOK
Local Phone (610) 941-9999
Fax (610) 941-9959

Printed in the United States of America

Printed on Recycled Paper

Published October 2005

Dedication

To Koko, my muse and good friend. And to her own special dog friends whose varied characters prompted this story: Bowser, Rosa, Piccolo, Juno, Sugar, Satchmo, Sammy, and Wili.

Acknowledgements

The author appreciates the dogs who—despite their impatience—let themselves be photographed for this book: Koko, Bowser, Rosa, Zoe, Gordita, Reeses, Sophie, Chester, Millie, Hatha and Easy.

The author is grateful to Paulette Frankl, photographer par excellence, who has such wonderful rapport with Koko, and took the front cover photograph, the photo of the author, the photos heading Chapters 4, 14, 18, 21, 23 and 27, and the photo on the last page. Thanks to other dog-loving photographers Karen Signell, Sue deWinter, Janice Sullivan and Lynn Lichtenwalter.

Much gratitude to Karen Signell, Marty and Bill Miller, Carol Bell, Karen Chamberlain and the community of writers in the Roaring Fork Valley for their helpful suggestions.

The Dogs of Shoretown

Koko

Bowser

Handsome

Rosa

Jenny

Piccolo

The Dogs of Porcupine City

Goldie

Toro

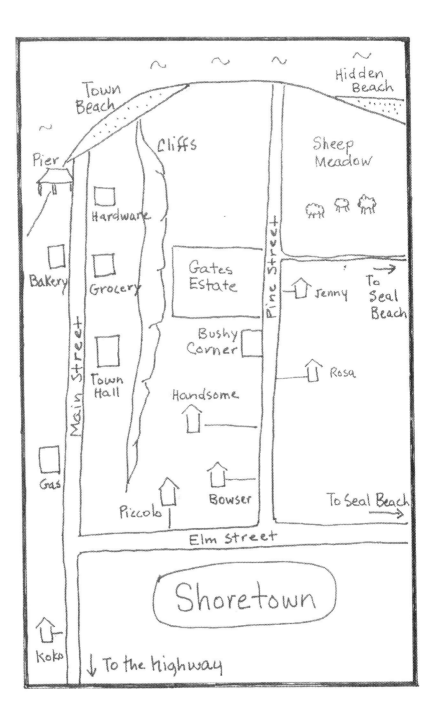

Chapter 1

Handsome had never been this scared. He tried to dig his claws into the dirt of the path, but the strange man dragged him deeper into the woods. From ahead came the whines and rapid barking of other dogs: thirsty, hungry, frightened dogs. Handsome's heart banged; his bladder trembled.

A small shed with boarded windows appeared through the trees, its tarpaper roof glittering in the sunlight.

The man dragged Handsome up to the door, unlocked it, pulled it open and shoved the black Lab inside into a mass of strong-smelling dogs. Handsome had hardly scrambled up when a large black and brown dog flew out of a dark corner. His powerful shoulder thudded against the man's chest. The man staggered, but held onto the door with one hand as the other seized the dog's leg.

The big dog crashed down. He strained to pull his muscled leg free. His strong body curved around to the hand on his leg, and his lips drew back to reveal his teeth. He growled.

"Bite the man. Hard!" one of the other dogs barked, but the big dog hesitated.

The man grabbed his collar, thrust him back into the shed and slammed the door. The room was suddenly dark. Handsome heard the lock snap shut and the man's footsteps recede.

"Why didn't you bite him, Master?" a dog whined.

"I couldn't." The big dog's tail went between his legs, and he slumped to the floor.

"So we can't escape, Master? Ever?" The big dog whimpered softly.

Handsome felt his heart plummet. He had never before been cruelly treated by humans. All his life he'd been loved, his instincts given free rein. But he was a dog of action rather than reflection. He did not wonder why he'd ended up in this foul pit. Instead, after signaling with his tail to the other dogs that he was no threat, he slumped down amongst them, closed his eyes and escaped into sleep.

Chapter 2

Just let her try to leash me. I'll drop her wallet in the toilet, Bowser vowed as he ran down the dirt road called Pine Street. He was a purebred wheaten terrier puppy, six months old, with curly white fur, a sturdy body, short tail and square face under cocked ears. He was still small enough to be picked up and cooed over by humans, something he felt was beneath his dignity.

He paused where the blackberry vines seemed densest, looked both ways—the road was empty—and ducked into the brush on a hidden path. Immediately before him, in the clearing known as Bushy Corner, half a dozen dogs stood in a circle, tails out. Bowser pushed his way in between little Piccolo and solid Jenny and saw lying in the dirt a picture of a black Lab with bright spots for eyes and a hanging tongue. Underneath were some human scribbles. The photo was of Handsome, Shoretown's most carefree dog, a dog so good-natured that he let Bowser and other puppies nip his ears and chase him.

"Lost," Jenny growled.

Lost! Bowser was stunned. Handsome, who raced down the beach and through the woods like a deer—*lost!* Not loping back home, his tongue hanging out? Not flirting with a coyote or visiting his human friends down the coast or gnawing at a huge bone in a nest of leaves?

"Maybe with two broken legs," Jenny barked, "or caught in a coyote trap."

Bowser whimpered, picturing Handsome, his leg clamped by toothed metal, weak from loss of blood, flies at his eyes. There were mountain lions in the woods. Stealthily, in the dark of night, a mountain lion would creep toward Handsome. The rustling breeze and the hooting owls would hide the sound of his lethal footsteps. Bowser lifted and lowered his paws silently.

"Some of you may be thinking *Wild Bunch*," Jenny went on. "You're hoping Handsome took it into his head to join them."

Bowser's heart leapt. He knew the legend: how the dogs of the Wild Bunch had left humans and gone to live free in the nearby woods like their ancestors, the wolves. They hunted game, bringing down only the sick and the weak and thus ensuring a steady supply of prey. It was said that they'd even brought down an occasional lamb in the sheep meadow. Bowser drooled. He saw clearly now: Handsome racing through the forest at the heart of a pack of swift dangerous beasts. "Yes," he barked, "I bet Handsome's joined the Wild Bunch."

"I don't think so," Jenny said. "Handsome's a Lab. He loves his humans and his food too much." The curly gray fur down her back stood up, and her thin cattle dog legs stood stiff. "He's been gone two days now. He was last seen at Seal Beach."

How did Jenny, the Shoretown dogs' alpha, know so much, Bowser wondered. Dominance lived in the brown eyes to either side of her gray blaze. Jenny was unique. Most dogs resembled at least one other dog. Some of them were experts at one thing, like Bowser and Piccolo, who were underground hunters, and Rosa, who was a water retriever. Some like Handsome, who was known both for his good nature and his strength, had a few talents.

But Jenny was all-in-one, what humans called *a mutt*. Bowser imagined that in her time Jenny had excelled at digging, retrieving, herding, guarding, pointing, swimming, racing and working with humans. Bowser admired her wide face and air of authority, chunky thin-legged body and coarse gray fur with black spots. Plus she smelled great. Her human, the mayor, respected her dog-ness and never made her smell of flowers.

"We must find him," Jenny went on. "Lots of humans don't like us being free. If we don't find Handsome, I'll bet my best bone the rest of us are going to get leashed."

Bowser joined the other dogs in loud barks of protest.

Jenny moved her powerful eyes from one dog to another. "We can't be leashed, can we, dogs?"

Together, the dogs howled their agreement.

"I know you'd all like to start looking for Handsome right away," Jenny continued, as Bowser exchanged expectant "Let's go" glances with the other dogs. "But we need to be organized and not running in every direction." Jenny raised her tail and bristled her fur. "I'm planning to ask Koko to head up the search."

"Koko!" Rosa's whine implied that no choice could have been stupider. She tossed her long silky spaniel ears. She was twice as big as Bowser, with a rich dark brown and white body and stub tail. Her whiskers quivered. "Koko's not a country dog. She's only been in Shoretown a few months. What does she know about finding Handsome?"

"She's a smart Australian shepherd," Jenny barked. "Plus, humans like her."

Bowser quivered with excitement watching this latest battle between Shoretown's two top dogs. Rosa, country cousin to prize-winning Springer spaniels, was the only dog in town who Jenny had trouble dominating.

"Koko's not at home in the country," Rosa pressed on. "Have you ever seen her relax and drift across a road without seeming to look? No, she's always checking both directions and then pat pat patting across as if she's at her human Michelle's heels. Does she know how to bring stones in from the ocean in her mouth? No. When Michelle tells her to come, have you ever seen her walk the other way? No."

Rosa looked around triumphantly at the others. "She may be a smart Aussie, but she's only a city dog."

"She's educated," Jenny barked.

Bowser, who liked the sound of the word *educated,* turned his small head to see what Rosa would answer to that.

"*Educated* just means *come, stay* and stuff like that," Rosa countered. "That's just learning to be a slave to humans."

That did it, Bowser thought. He never wanted to be *educated.*

A growl rumbled under Jenny's next words. "The other day Michelle was in front of the bakery and called Koko to come across the street. Koko saw a car that Michelle hadn't noticed, and she stayed put. She's not at all a slave to humans. She uses intelligent disobedience."

Intelligent disobedience. Bowser liked the sound of both words.

Rosa looked away and raised a paw in defeat.

"Plus," Jenny went on, pressing her advantage, "being trusted by humans never hurt a dog. I'm going to talk to Koko as soon as she gets off work."

Chapter 3

When the puppy Bowser reached home, his human, Daisy, was in the front yard wielding long garden clippers. She was mutilating the pink starflower vines that had wound their way over the neighbor's garage into her yard. No matter how pretty or fragrant a flower might be, Daisy didn't like it just arriving on its own.

When she saw Bowser, she set down the clippers, reached out her hand as if it contained a treat and called, "Come here, sweetie. Here's a treat." Over her soft curvy body, she wore a purple dress with red flowers and in her fluffy brown hair two silver clips shone like stars.

Bowser hesitated. Mixed with the usual morning smells of fresh bread and coffee was no smell of treat. Instead, he smelled something else. While his human sounded as if all she wanted was to feed and hug him, he could smell her other intent: to take him to that awful place where he was to be nearly drowned, de-scented, re-scented, strapped to a contraption, fur-chopped and sprayed until he smelled like a rose and looked like a stuffed toy. Once in his six-month lifetime had been enough. Did he have to go through that again?

"Bowser," she wheedled.

He yearned toward her voice and smell. He wanted to jump into her arms. He loved her, for she was his human mother now that his dog mother had vanished. But Bowser backed away.

"Come on, honey."

Daisy came closer. Her smell of deceit was stronger. Her round face was huge. She was about to catch and leash him, maybe forever. As she lunged, Bowser's teeth came together in a sharp click, just missing her fingers.

She cried out.

He turned and raced away.

At first he was elated, the wind tousling his wiry white fur as his small feet galloped over the dirt road, rutted with car tracks and dried-up puddles. He had taken action, not let himself be led into a cage like a sheep. He had been oblivious to his human's faults when he'd chosen her at eight weeks, but now she seemed devious as a cat. She was nothing like Jenny.

Snapping at a human . . . Bowser slowed. He whimpered softly. When Jenny had gone over the Tooth Code last week, he'd been chewing a stolen potholder stained with pork fat and hadn't paid enough attention. Snapping at another dog wasn't bad. There were occasions that called for it. But snapping at a human . . . Bowser quailed.

If his teeth had touched her fingers, it might have been called a *bite*. No dog could bite a human and get away with it. His human was a soft person who liked everything under control. To her, *snapping* might be as frightening as *biting*. Much as she loved him, much as she cried her heart out for him, she might be even now arranging for the sheriff to take him away.

Bowser ran blindly down the long path toward Seal Beach, ignoring the burrs and twigs that caught in his fur and the nagging thorns in his mind. If he could only find a clue to where Handsome had gone, maybe she'd forgive and forget his mistake. A dog who rescued one of his kind was not heralded by other dogs (it was expected dog behavior), but humans fell over themselves in admiration.

As he emerged onto the sunlit beach, a strange hawk-like bird with a creamy belly flew toward him, almost grazing his head with a long wing. The falcon alighted nearby to peck at a piece of driftwood. Bowser narrowed his eyes. The bird smelled a little like a human—how odd. Odd too that she was on the beach. Usually all he saw were gulls and shore birds. Plus, no other hawk-like bird had ever let Bowser get this close.

The falcon was looking right at him, a challenge in her yellow-ringed eyes.

Bowser pricked his ears forward and crouched. His muscles tensed. *All right, you asked for it*, he barked. His four feet left the ground and came down hard, right where the falcon had been the instant before. The puppy's nose brushed the tip of her wing as the bird flew up into the air and down the beach.

He raced after her, his little legs wind-milling over the sand. He could almost feel that trembling feathery life in his mouth. The bird was tiring, Bowser could tell.

Suddenly, she veered inland, and Bowser took after her. They flew over the dunes and down a sandy path toward some nearby trees. The bird's gleaming brown tail was inches from the puppy's nose as they tore from the sunlight into the woods. Bowser blinked as things darkened, and he put on an extra burst of speed.

Too late, he saw the bird, with a sudden pulse of one wing, veer into the oak leaves above him. Too late, he saw the outline of the van with its open back doors. He tried to brake, but his speed propelled him forward up a ramp and into the dark insides of the van.

Bowser's claws scraped on the ridged metal floor as he tried to turn and escape. But in that instant, a cigarette-smelling man jumped into the van behind him. Bowser felt his squirming body grabbed hard, and his new collar unbuckled and pulled off. The man heaved him into a corner of the van. Before Bowser could scramble to his feet, the man was out, and the two metal doors had clanged shut.

The terrier stood listening. The van didn't move. Outside, there was a rustling of brush that gradually grew softer and disappeared. The man's scent faded. Silence descended.

Bowser started shaking. So this was what happened to a dog who snapped at his human!

Daisy must have sent this awful man to capture him. Was he to be abandoned to die here in this van in the woods? Bowser cocked his head to the side in the way she liked and gazed in the direction of home, telling her, *I'm sorry. I'll never do it again. Please don't leave me to die.*

Soon his neck felt sore. He curled up on the ribs of the metal floor, so all he could smell was his puppy self. Birds cheeped outside. Why had he chased that stupid bird? If he hadn't done that, he wouldn't be here now. That stupid bird . . . Bowser closed his eyes.

He woke at the noise of the van's front door closing. The engine coughed, caught and broke into a rumble, and the puppy slid a little across the metal floor as the van began to move. A vision of various horribles came to him. What if Daisy had arranged for him to be left alone in the middle of the woods with a dead chicken tied around his neck? He'd heard that had happened once to a farm dog.

Bowser trembled as the van bumped over the uneven ground. He scrunched down to peer through the crack of light under the door, but he could see nothing.

Now the van was turning onto a paved road. Probably they'd be going close to town. Someone might hear him. In his dark cage Bowser lifted his head and howled with all his might.

Chapter 4

Koko leapt suddenly to her feet: Was that faint howl Bowser's? Through the open French windows she glimpsed a beat-up gray van gliding past. Koko's small brown nose quivered, and her thick copper-red fur stood on end. A complicated smell of burnt oil, dried liver treats and bird droppings entered her Aussie brain, already crammed with scents, instincts, rules, a hundred words of English and a powerful dog vocabulary.

Koko glanced toward Michelle, who sat nearby in a wooden rocking chair gazing toward their therapy patient, Mrs. Gates. Every weekday morning Koko helped Michelle in her work of honoring other humans, which meant sharing their emotions and comforting them. Ever since Michelle and Koko had moved to Shoretown, they'd worked together in this quiet airy room with its polished oak floor, colorful rugs and dark furniture.

Serious Koko loved and respected serious Michelle, and the Aussie knew it was wrong of her to interrupt the therapy hour. Still, she stood gazing at Michelle in her fox-colored cardigan. Michelle seemed completely focused on the watchful, sweet-smelling woman sitting on the couch.

"Down, Koko," Michelle said, holding a palm up—it was the signal that Koko was to lie down again. Koko tried to bore through to Michelle with her eyes. That faint howling of Bowser's from the passing van was important. Maybe nobody else had heard it. Couldn't Koko be excused from work to go notify her alpha, Jenny? She wasn't really needed here—Mrs. Gates seemed fine. Wasn't it true that the violet fragrance that Mrs. Gates wore these days was preferable to the strong cloud of alcohol that had clung to her a month ago?

"Down," Michelle repeated in her heartfelt Koko-PLEASE-be-my-buddy voice, and then "Good dog," as Koko sank back, pushed away her worries about Bowser and turned her attention again toward Mrs. Gates.

"I expect she'd rather be out gallivanting," the small woman with the soft wrinkled skin remarked.

"Do you think so?" Michelle asked in her clear consulting-room voice, the one that sounded like brook water. "What do you think she'd like to be doing?"

"Something naughty, I expect. In the old days, the dogs in town were always nosing around my father's salmon cannery. Perhaps she'd—" Mrs. Gates stopped talking. Her brow furrowed, and her chin trembled. "That reminds me. I visited my daughter in the city a few nights ago and she served me *fish* for dinner." Her face twisted into a pug-like expression, her nose wrinkled.

Koko cocked her head in puzzlement. Didn't Mrs. Gates know that *fish*—that was one of the human words Michelle had taught her—was delicious? True, you had to watch out for bones, but a fish, not too long dead, found on the beach, was a special treat. Plus, if it was too dead to eat, you could always roll on it.

"I grew up having to smell that awful cannery night and day, and I've never gotten over it. Even the freshest fish can make me quite queasy. And here my daughter has completely forgotten."

Mrs. Gates repeated in a wavering voice, "Completely forgotten." Tears ran down her powdered cheeks, and Koko, feeling Michelle touch her lightly, hurried over to put her front feet on the couch and stretch up to this human, trying to reassure her.

12

"Oh, my dear," Mrs. Gates said, awkwardly reaching to hug Koko with her bony arms. "You wouldn't forget your old Mum hated fish, would you, even if she had her faults?" Koko tasted a salt tear on Mrs. Gates' soft cheek, plus chemicals and violets.

Mrs. Gates pulled back and searched Koko's eyes. At that moment Koko gave her heart to the unhappy woman, all her love for humans pouring out in her gaze.

Once Mrs. Gates seemed calm, Koko returned to her co-therapist's place on the rug.

As the two women went on talking, she lay licking her paw, haunted again by Bowser's cry for help from the van. Outside a truck rumbled past pulling the grocery store dumpster off to the dump near the highway. Koko's nose twitched at the food aromas from it.

Then she flattened her ears in anxiety and felt her paws moist with sweat as she realized she would no longer be able to track the van: the dumpster would have overlaid its smells. Her whiskers quivered as she tried to recall the van's aromas and sort them out from spoiled food. There'd been something else familiar in that smell. Very faint, troubling.

The van had smelled of Handsome!

Koko stopped licking and concentrated. Had it been Handsome—swamp, hoof and seal—or was she imagining his scent, like a love struck pup?

Not that the Lab was much of a dog, to her way of thinking. All he wanted to do was have fun. You wouldn't catch Handsome herding stray humans on a walk or teaching puppies some tedious lesson like when and where to pee.

Still, there'd been that unforgettable moment on the beach two mornings ago. By running fast Koko had always been able to break through into bliss, leave ordinary things behind and hurl herself into the bright wild *Neverendingness*. Usually she was alone in that world, but the other day Handsome had been there too, streaking along beside her. It had been a wonderful feeling, but also disturbing, that shimmering black shape so close by.

Later, when they'd spotted Koko's human, Michelle, on the beach, Handsome had raced over and jumped up with his paws on her chest, almost knocking Michelle over. It must have been his exuberance, his love of life. Maybe he'd wanted to say, "I like Koko and I like *you* too."

But Michelle hadn't understood. She'd said, "Down," raising her hand in the *Down* signal, and Handsome had just jumped higher, thinking she had a treat for him. His teeth must have grazed her hand because she'd cried, "Watch it, you big lug," in a startled voice.

That cry from dear Michelle had been like a splintered bone in Koko's heart. Now she felt ashamed of what she'd done next. She'd barked at Handsome, "Michelle's right, you are a big lug." Then she'd turned her back on him and trotted off with Michelle. That had been two days ago and she hadn't seen him since.

Not for two days . . . Koko licked her paw again nervously. Handsome might be an oaf and a wastrel, but he was also strong as a horse, brave as a raccoon and sweet and spicy as a ginger snap. She was not about to let anything bad happen to him.

The town dogs' alpha, Jenny, must be informed that Handsome and Bowser had been stolen by a man in a van. Standing up, Koko went to the closed door and stared at it. Just as she'd hoped, Michelle responded, and Koko went racing down the hall, through the kitchen, flipping through her dog door and galloping off toward Pine Street.

Koko stared with sinking heart at the picture of Handsome the other dogs had left in the dirt at Bushy Corner. She placed her paw on his cheek.

"There you are," came Jenny's gruff voice from behind her. "I thought you worked until noon."

Koko turned to see Jenny's sturdy body outlined against the blackberry bushes. "I got off early," Koko said, averting her gaze in a quick deferential gesture. Her eyes snapped back to Jenny's. "I've got news," she barked.

"Speak."

"Bowser's been stolen. Maybe Handsome too."

Jenny sat down suddenly in the dust, as if Koko's words had weakened her backbone.

"By a man in an old van."

Jenny's fur bristled.

Her body trembling, her paws poised to run, Koko told the alpha about the van and the dumpster. She waited for Jenny to spring into action, assemble the other Shoretown dogs and start an immediate search. Although how they would search now that the trail was overlaid . . . well, that was Jenny's problem.

"Sit down, Koko."

If ever Koko came close to disobeying her alpha, it was now. But she sat and flattened her ears in submission.

"I've been watching you since you moved to town and I've concluded you're a very competent intelligent dog. You Aussies can be excitable, but the alarm you're showing now is justified."

This was all well and good. Koko liked a compliment as well as any dog. But now wasn't the time for it. Her muscles itched to be moving.

"I would like to ask you to head up the investigation into the disappearance of Handsome and Bowser. All us Shoretown dogs will be available to help but I want you to be in charge."

"Me?" Koko's mind whirled. *I'll try to find—no, I'll get all the dogs together—no.* Was this any way for Jenny to treat a newcomer, unload this difficult task on her? Should Koko say she had swallowed a wasp by accident and could not think straight?

"You're the right dog for this, but if you don't want to do it, I'll ask Rosa." Jenny's black ears stood up as she stared at Koko.

"Not Rosa!" Koko barked. Rosa was smart and able, but Koko couldn't stand the spaniel's superior airs and sarcastic snarls. "She'd be no good for the job at all." No, Koko thought, she would not let Rosa have the job she herself was born to. Wasn't she a herder, the natural one to find the stolen dogs and herd them back to town? Now she saw why Jenny had picked her. "The first thing," she barked, "is to go to town and find Piccolo. He can be on the alert for the van."

"Good thinking," Jenny agreed, and the two of them trotted out from Bushy Corner and back down Pine Street.

Chapter 5

As the van barreled along farther and farther from Shoretown, Bowser slumped with an aching heart, scenes from the past in his mind's eye. He remembered lying with his three tiny sisters and two brothers on some green grass, watching a shiny fly go by but being too sleepy to go after it. He remembered his human when he'd first seen her, round eyes and a round mouth, how she'd reached out her warm finger to touch him on the tip of his nose and said, "I'll take this little guy." He remembered the first time he'd chewed a dried pig's ear, how he'd licked it at first and then tentatively tried to bite it, and the thrill he'd felt when it cracked sharply.

The van tilted rounding a curve, and Bowser skidded across the floor into a corner. His nose quivered. Other dogs had been back here. Why hadn't he noticed that before? Handsome had been here. Was this perhaps a grooming truck?

Bowser pictured dozens of dogs like himself tied to contraptions while their fur was chopped with scissors and pulled at with combs and sprayed with glue, their ears were tunneled into with sticks, their nails blunted and their teeth assaulted. Maybe, if that were to be his fate, he could contact the others by some mystical means and they would all, at the same moment, tear out their restraints and light out for the woods to join the Wild Bunch.

Maybe the Wild Bunch would give him a prize for—but Bowser stopped himself. The Wild Bunch was not going to give bones to a dog who in dangerous circumstances did nothing but lie around and dream of receiving them. The Wild Bunch dogs were desperate characters. They would never award a prize to a do-nothing dog.

Say instead of Bowser, the man had trapped the Wild Bunch. Bowser could almost see them in the darkness, lithe rangy dogs with sleek muscled bodies who smelled like dead seal. They'd be chewing an escape hole in the side of the van right now with their strong-as-iron teeth. Bowser tried to get a grip on one of the metal ridges along the wall, but his teeth slid right off. He tried again, pressing himself against the wall, his neck at an awkward angle. This time his teeth remained where they were.

Harder and harder he bit until his jaws started aching and his mouth trembled, but the metal gave only the tiniest bit. His teeth had made only two dents so small he could hardly find them when he tried to reposition himself on the constantly tilting floor.

The puppy gave up and staggered around the speeding van, sniffing. If he couldn't gnaw his way out, he'd have to escape some other way. There were no weak spots in the walls or floor. The place was as bare and strong as a vet's cage. His only chance to escape was when the man opened the back doors. Bowser studied the door latch. The man would open the right-hand door with one hand and reach in with the other to grab Bowser. If he was close to the door, he was sure to get caught, but if he stayed back, the man would have to climb into the van and Bowser might have a chance to scoot by him.

But the man was fast and strong. It would help if he thought catching Bowser would be easy. It would help if he thought Bowser was asleep. Bowser remembered the day he'd seen a possum lying on some leaves and no matter how he'd pushed at it with his nose and paws, the possum had stayed limp. Bowser had gotten bored and left, but when he went by that bunch of leaves a little while later the possum was gone. He couldn't believe it. Then something had made him look up, and there was the possum's naked little face watching him through the leaves.

The possum had made a fool of him and he would do exactly the same to the man. Bowser strutted around the van, managing to keep his balance, his head high. If Handsome or Jenny could see him now, would they be impressed!

The van made a right turn and started up a winding road with no scents of cars or people, just wild animals and birds.

When the vehicle stopped, Bowser slid a few yards and for a moment stood stupidly. Then the puppy rushed to his corner and lay down, closing his eyes as if asleep. He heard the van's front door open and a little later close. Again they were moving. Bowser raised his head, listened with cocked ears and sniffed warily.

The van stopped again, and this time the engine died. Bowser lowered his head. He kept his eyes slitted so he could watch the door, and, just as he'd expected, the right hand door opened, a wedge of light fell in and the top half of the man appeared against the bright outdoors. "Get over here." The man had a brisk sharp voice, like a crow's.

Bowser didn't move. He fluttered his lashes slightly so he could keep his eyes on the man.

The man reached a hand into his clothes. When he brought it out, the aroma of dried liver treat thwacked Bowser hard. No fair! Any dog, smelling dried liver treat, would have opened his eyes and looked up hungrily, just like Bowser. He could see enough against the light to tell the man was holding out a nice big chunk.

"That woke you, did it? Come on, this is for you."

Bowser considered. The dried liver smelled awfully good, and the fact the man was offering it meant he wasn't all bad.

The man pulled himself up into the van and, crouching, came toward Bowser, arms out.

Just before the grasping hands reached him, Bowser dashed between the man's legs, leaped out of the van and lost himself in the brush as fast as he could.

Bowser was not sure just where he was. He had barged through thickets, almost strangled himself in vines and finally found a path out in the open. The man would never catch him, he vowed, even if he had to run until he dropped dead. Which might be soon, he thought, his chest was stinging so bitterly. Either way, his human, Daisy, whom he could not help yearning for, would be lost to him forever. What kind of miserable creature was he, to have snapped like that at the one he loved most?

There was no one around, but he had the odd feeling someone was watching him. Maybe the dogs of the Wild Bunch were admiring him from those woods over there, discussing how to ask him to join them.

But then the puppy's ears flattened and he hunched lower as it occurred to him he wasn't being watched from the woods, but from above. Bowser tried to look up as he ran, tripped, banged his nose on a rock, and finally stopped, peering up anxiously. There was nothing in the sky but a tiny speck. He looked in all directions. The sky was clear blue: nothing in it but that speck. His paws were sweating from the sensation of being watched. He narrowed his eyes. The sky was very bright. Sometimes it seemed like he imagined that speck, that it was just one of those spots he saw when he looked too close to the sun. But the speck remained.

And grew bigger as Bowser cowered, mesmerized. The speck came plummeting down toward him as fast as a car, its wings beating fast. It had fierce eyes and a hooked beak. Bowser turned around and took off running the way he'd come. He could hear the monster rushing through the air right behind him. Ahead was a ditch—he leapt over it. Around him bursts of blue and yellow flowers swept by. Another ditch, a fallen tree. He dared not look back. All he could hear was the *ssshh* sound of the monster chasing him.

Any moment its talons would dig into his back. What could he do? He'd be pecked to pieces. Suddenly before him were two humans, the man who'd seized him and an older woman. They were standing beside the gray van and a big stone house. The puppy streaked down the dirt path toward them, dived between the man's legs and stopped, pressing against the man's ragged jeans, smelling his familiar cigarette smell.

The man laughed and pulled him roughly around by the neck fur. Bowser panted hard and peered back down the path toward the monster, but it was nowhere in sight.

The woman talking to the man had cropped gray hair, long pants and a blouse with pictures of birds on it. She had laughed when Bowser appeared, but now she was watching something on the man's shoulder. Bowser craned his head to follow her gaze. There, looking as cool as seawater, settling her wings next to the man's face, was the same arrogant bird he'd chased at the beach. Bowser barked in protest. The bird cast her cold glance on him, and his paws began to sweat, just as they had when the monster had chased him. Was this bird the monster? Bowser growled low. The bird looked down at him and opened her sharp curved beak. Bowser whimpered.

With the hand that wasn't gripping Bowser's neck fur, the man reached into his jeans pocket and took out a dried liver treat. Well, even if he was caught, at least he'd be fed now, Bowser thought, drooling.

But the man gave the treat to the bird. A bird wasn't supposed to get dried liver treats, they were meant for dogs! The bird gulped it down without ceremony. What's more, the man, at the same time he gripped Bowser's neck painfully, *stroked* the bird's throat with his other hand, and said, in the same heartfelt way Bowser's human used to talk to him, "Good Kharma, good bird." It wasn't fair.

"I still say that's no life for a falcon," the woman said.

"She's free to go." Still holding Bowser, the man moved to the front of the van and took from the seat a leash and dog collar with a small black box hitched to it. As he tightened the bulky collar around Bowser's neck, the bird, still on the man's shoulder, stared at the puppy with dark eyes. The bird had yellow on its face and a hooked beak, just like the monster. But she was only a medium-sized bird, nowhere near as big as the monster. Still . . . Bowser looked away and lowered his stance.

"You know perfectly well she isn't free to go," the woman said. "You've played with her mind. You've tamed her with your treats and fussing. A bird like that should be riding the winds a mile up. If you truly loved her, you'd wean her from you and let her go free."

During this speech the man had stood up and moved, tugging Bowser along, to a large wire cage a few feet off the ground. He opened its door, and carefully, with a few sweet murmurs, moved the bird from his shoulder to a perch inside the cage. "I know how you feel, Mom," he said wearily. "You've told me enough times. Now I've got to put this dog away."

The woman's eyes when she looked down at Bowser were stern and a little frightened. "How many of them do you have down there?"

"A couple." Bowser could feel that the man wanted to get away from her, but she seemed to be the alpha, and he was held by her questions.

"And how many have you already returned to their homes?"

"Eight or nine." Bowser could smell deceit: the man was lying.

"Is that the truth, Andrew?"

His voice grew firmer and more deceitful. "I've trained nine dogs not to chase birds and returned those dogs to their homes."

"Good for you." But the woman still held him there. Bowser sensed her love for the man struggle with her distrust. "When did you take them back?"

His voice was defensive. "A few the week before last, three last weekend. Another Thursday afternoon, one yesterday."

You know he's lying, Bowser whimpered to the woman. *Take your authority and throw him to the ground.*

The woman hesitated. Bowser urged her on, but he felt her instead suddenly submit, as if she were not the alpha at all. "Well, that's a relief. I was picturing that shed filling up with dogs. So your electric shock machine is working?"

"Like a charm."

They stood in silence. Bowser could sense the strain between them. Then the woman took a deep breath, clapped her hands together and said, "I found another nest of western bluebirds, quite close by."

"That's great, Mom."

"I'll get back to them."

"Sure."

Now the man turned on his heel and started down a gravel path. Bowser trotted along beside him on the leash, the box on the strange collar poking into his throat. Soon the path became dirt and descended in a winding way through woods. Birds, raccoon, skunk, possum and deer lived here. It was just like Bowser imagined the Wild Bunch's land would be. He heard the faint rush of water. Now he smelled Handsome. There were other dogs too. He could smell their pee and mawna. Bowser leapt ahead and felt the leash stop him with a jerk.

"You'll be there soon enough," the man said.

As they walked, the sound of water crashing grew louder. Bowser saw a wooden shed standing on the opposite bank of a swift creek. Water cascaded down over rocks in a long rush. Bowser cocked his ears in excitement. Under the noise of the waterfall, Handsome was barking from inside. Other dogs barked too.

But there were also hungry whines and frightened yelps among the barks. Something was wrong. Bowser stopped and pulled back against the leash in dismay.

The man dragged the puppy across a bridge of old boards. He unlocked a gate into a fenced yard, pulled Bowser through and redid the lock. With a lunge, Bowser yanked the leash out of the man's hand and raced around the noisy shed, only to skid to a stop where the fence met the building. "Gotcha," the man said, as his foot came down on the leash.

At the door of the shed, he bent to grab Bowser by the collar and undo the leash. Then he pulled open the door a crack. There was a moment when all was confusion. Bowser saw a dog's barking face, another, felt himself thrust through the narrow opening into a strange dog's side, smelled a great wave of pee and mawna, felt the slam of the door and the light disappear.

Immediately, in the dimness and stench of the room, a big brown and black dog loomed over the puppy. The dog's black lip lifted. A growl rumbled in his massive chest. Bowser quickly rolled onto his back and looked aside in submission. The big dog placed a paw on his stomach and sniffed him all over. Bowser trembled. Shortly, the dog stalked away.

Bowser, still prone, lifted his head slightly and glanced around. He could barely make out nine dogs in the shed. As he recognized his friend, he barked, "Handsome!"

But before Handsome could reply, the puppy felt a great weight press his body down, a weight so heavy he could hardly breathe. Dog fur and flesh were in his mouth, his nostrils and his eyes. He struggled for air. His sense of the other dogs faded.

Just before he lost consciousness, he realized what had happened. The big brown and black dog was alpha and had decided to sit down on him.

Chapter 6

While many of the Shoretown dogs lived on the windy mesa, which stretched along the coast a hundred feet above the ocean, the downtown area was tucked in the bottom of a gully. Koko and Jenny decided against scooting to town the fast way down a crumbly dirt cliff. Instead they took dusty Pine Street and sloping Elm to Main. That way, whenever they spotted a dog, Koko could stop to ask questions: When had the dog last seen Handsome? Bowser?

The answers were disappointing. No one had spotted Handsome since he'd headed for Seal Beach two mornings ago. As for Bowser the answers were: "Yesterday," "This morning, at Bushy Corner," "Last week," "Can't remember."

Koko and Jenny passed the gas station, the town hall and the community free box, their noses twitching as they caught whiffs of butter from the bakery. They trotted up to the wide board porch outside the grocery store and its hundred delicious smells: beef, pork, peanut butter, cheese, chocolate.

Piccolo, the Jack Russell terrier, was usually to be found on this porch since his humans ran the store, but it was vacant at the moment. Jenny led Koko around the building to an empty dumpster standing on wooden ties.

Jenny sniffed under the dumpster. "Piccolo?"

"Mmmmrffff."

"Get out here. Koko needs to tell you something. Leave that rat alone."

A small brown and white head appeared from under the dumpster, followed by a dusty white body. Piccolo blinked dirt out of his eyes. "I was just about to fight him. But that's okay. What do you want, Jenny?"

"You're to stay on the porch from now on," Jenny ordered. "Now come back around with us."

The three dogs trotted around the building and up to the porch. Koko liked the terrier Piccolo. He had the same kind of energy as she did. She could sense he wanted action.

"You've been after that rat for months," Jenny growled.

"That was a different one. I caught that one. But what do rats matter? Does Koko need my expertise?" Piccolo asked. "I can bark, dig, chase, hunt, destroy—whatever you need."

"You don't have to do any of that," Koko said. "Just stay on this porch every day—"

Piccolo yelped with disappointment.

"Just stay on this porch every day," Koko repeated, "and let us know if a certain van comes by. If the man who took Handsome and Bowser lives around here, he might come to your store to buy food. I saw and smelled the van earlier. It's a gray van smelling of Bowser, Handsome, a young white human male, filter cigarettes, falcon droppings, dried liver, burnt oil, leather boots, salmon steaks, beach sand, epoxy glue, Pepsi, dried-up French fries and chewing gum."

For a moment, Piccolo looked stunned. Then he said, "Yes, Koko." His nose quivered, his small dark terrier eyes scanned the vehicles in sight suspiciously. "I do smell some cigarette smoke."

"If the van were here, I would have already recognized it, wouldn't I?" Koko asked him.

"It could be in disguise," Piccolo said.

After Koko and Jenny had left Piccolo on duty at the grocery store, they arranged to meet again after lunch. It was common dog knowledge that whenever Ranger Bill visited Koko and Michelle's house for a meal, Koko must be home. He didn't like dogs bothering his wild deer and foxes, and it was Koko's job to reassure him by appearing to lie around the house all day.

The Aussie raced back, slicing through the rosemary bushes in the side garden just as Ranger Bill's white pick-up truck crunched into Michelle's gravel driveway. Koko hesitated. She had hoped Ranger Bill might have learned of the dog stealing, but she could sense no upset in him. She ran around the house and slipped in her dog door.

As Koko entered the kitchen, Michelle turned from the stove to crouch and greet her. Michelle's familiar toasty smell enveloped Koko, and her strong hands kneaded Koko's neck muscles. "Sweetie, I was scared you wouldn't make it back in time. What a good dog you are."

Koko sank down on the linoleum and gave little grunts of pleasure at Michelle's firm touch.

"You were so great this morning with Mrs. Gates. I don't know what I'd do without you."

"Honey, I got us some brownies for dessert." Ranger Bill, who had come in the front door, appeared in the sunny kitchen. He was a big smiling man with thick brown hair, arms like cougars and a belly that poked out over the thick belt of his ranger uniform.

"Oh, Bill, you promised you wouldn't buy any more of that fattening stuff," Michelle chided as she stood up and turned her face to kiss him.

After Ranger Bill and Michelle had hugged and kissed, he crouched down to scratch Koko roughly all up and down her body. She grunted, loving his hands on her, his deep voice and smell of pinesap. "How's my Kokomo? You know, Michelle, if I hadn't got to know Koko—her being such a responsible dog—damned if I wouldn't vote for that leash law on Friday."

"How can you even say such a thing?" Michelle turned toward Ranger Bill, holding aloft her soup ladle, which Koko watched for drips. "You couldn't do that. You love animals too much."

"I don't know." Bill sat down and bent over to smell a loaf of crusty bread on the table. "I've been lobbied pretty hard lately. That Mrs. Nightingale I told you about must have called me a dozen times in the last few months. 'The poor snowy plovers,' 'the poor great blue herons,' 'the poor terns.' It's a wonder we have any birds left, according to her." His next words were spoken in such a funny high voice that Koko gave him a startled glance. "That's why you must pass a leash law in Shoretown, Bill. It's the last town on the coast without one."

"That sounds just like Mrs. Nightingale." Michelle banged the ladle on the edge of the soup pan.

Nightingale. There was a new word. Koko sensed Michelle didn't like it, whatever it meant. And there was the word *birds*, and the bad word *leash*.

Michelle was silent as she ladled soup into blue bowls and brought them to the table. "Mrs. Nightingale doesn't even live here," she burst out. "Doesn't she have some mansion up the coast?"

"It's no use arguing with Mrs. Nightingale. She's not one to change her mind." Ranger Bill took a spoonful of green soup with bits of ham in it and swallowed with pleasure. Koko watched enviously. "Anyhow, she may be distracted over the next few weeks. I saw her son Andrew's old van out near Seal Beach this morning."

Koko sat up. Ranger Bill had just said *Seal Beach.* Handsome had disappeared there. Ranger Bill knew something.

"I didn't know she had a son," Michelle said, sitting down and tearing a chunk of bread from the loaf.

"Oh, yeah. Andrew's a strange bird himself, a chip off the old block. He's been working up in Canada with one of those activist groups who lie down in front of bulldozers or something. I guess he's visiting his mother."

28

Koko stood up and wagged her rear end in anticipation. Soon Ranger Bill would say *Handsome*, he'd smell upset, and she'd know he understood.

But she waited in vain.

Chapter 7

In an unconscious fog, squashed under the big brown and black dog, Bowser remembered a scene from the very beginning of his life. From a warm, cramped place he'd come forth to a new world with a squeeze, a pop and a gasping intake of air. A vast space had suddenly swelled around him, and a hot tongue had tumbled him upside down and around, causing him to wiggle with delight.

But a moment later all that had changed. A great weight had pressed him down; fur had been in his mouth and nose. He hadn't been able to breathe. He had struggled, trying to find that great space again. He'd felt a bursting feeling as if he might explode. Bowser had flexed all his tiny muscles, but he'd been weak as a bubble under his mother.

Then the big dog's weight suddenly lifted, and Bowser struggled out of unconsciousness to breathe. He gave a strangled cough.

Tall and big chested, the dog thrust his muzzle toward Bowser. "Quiet, Pup. I am Toro, Master here. You'll obey me in all things."

Bowser rolled on his back, flattened his little ears and looked around. His first thought was that he'd died, and this was some afterworld of punishment. The ten-by-ten shed was dark, its windows boarded over. The air was stifling and filled with the buzzing of flies, the stench of pee and mawna, and the panting of dogs.

Hearing the splash of the waterfall he felt parched and stood up cautiously to look for a water dish. The seven dogs besides Toro and Handsome were a dirty golden retriever, a shepherd, two long-legged hounds and three dogs like Jenny. They lay immobile amongst the tufts of fur and stains on the wood floor. Flies walked around on the dogs undisturbed. All of them had collars with boxes on them like Bowser's, and they all lay on their sides, panting, their eyes on Toro.

"You can lie over there near the privy," Toro said, indicating a back corner of the shed. Bowser picked his way through the dogs, who raised their heads in greeting.

It was hard to tell what these dogs were feeling. Their coats were dirty, some of their ribs showed through, many had bloody hot spots on their front legs, and one of the hounds shivered continuously despite the heat. But their eyes flashed with life.

Bowser lay down carefully near a big pile of mawna, then wriggled to a better spot between Handsome and the golden retriever. Toro eyed him but said nothing until Bowser snapped at a fly.

"No snapping," Toro said.

Bowser stared at the big dog in amazement. "He doesn't let us move?" he whimpered to Handsome.

Toro's eyes blazed, and he stalked toward Bowser.

Handsome warned, "He's having a hard day. Apologize and call him *Master* a lot." Dogs scrambled out of Toro's way. In seconds, he was looming over Bowser, his lip curled.

"What were you conspiring about just now?"

"I wasn't, Master. I'm sorry, Master. I won't do it again, Master." Bowser rolled on his back and looked aside, trembling under Toro's fierce eyes.

The alpha's rank breath struck Bowser's face, and a drop of Toro's saliva landed in Bowser's eye. Flies landed and walked around on his furless stomach, and the box on his collar poked him. But the puppy struggled to keep from moving.

"Troops, how long since we've had water and food?" Toro raised his head and howled.

"Two days," the other dogs, raising their heads, chorused.

"How long since we've been allowed in the yard?"

"Two days!"

"What's the longest any dog's been here?"

"Eighteen days!"

"Will our humans save us?"

"No!"

"Are we giving up?"

"No!" The dogs scrambled to their feet.

"Who's going to lead you out of here?"

"You, Master!"

"Who almost gave his life to set you free?"

"You, Master!"

"Who's going to come up with a perfect plan of escape?"

"You, Master!" the dogs howled.

Toro returned to his post at the right of the door, the prime spot in the shed. He sat down regally, his head turning this way and that to survey the others. For a moment he was quiet, but then he stood up nervously and began to pace around the shed, the other dogs crowding against each other as they cleared a path.

He stalked around, snapping when a dog didn't move fast enough, mounting one of the hounds who cowered under him, her tail between her legs, until he growled angrily at her and moved away. Bowser had to jump aside three times before Toro returned to his place.

The big dog lay down and lowered his chin onto his front paws. In a moment the others sensed from his breathing that he was asleep.

As the other dogs turned their attention to their infected legs, the buzzing of flies mixed with the rasping sounds of dry tongues against fur. Outside the waterfall splashed. "Toro sure is mean," Bowser low-barked to Handsome. "Much meaner than Rosa."

"I hear he used to be fair," Handsome said. "But the day I came, he tried to lead an escape, and it didn't work, and he's been mean ever since. Tell me," Handsome's pleading brown eyes peered into Bowser's. "Have you seen my humans?"

"Not lately."

Handsome whimpered, "They've probably found another dog."

"Oh, no, Handsome," the puppy assured him. "I saw a picture of you they made. There were tear stains on it."

Handsome brightened and wagged his tail. "Really?"

The golden retriever on the other side of Bowser muttered in a bitter voice, "Enjoy it while you can. It's only a matter of time before your humans betray you."

"This is Goldie," Handsome told Bowser, "from Porcupine City down the coast. They used to be free like us, but their humans leashed them a while ago. She was captured by the bad man long before me. Isn't that right, Goldie?"

The golden closed and opened her hurt eyes in assent. Her face had the soft noble lines of her kind, but her red-gold fur was clotted with bits of mawna and spit.

"If they leash us in Shoretown," Bowser growled, pulling his lips back from his little teeth, "I'm going to revolt."

"Yes, Pup, we thought the same," Goldie said. "But humans are stronger than dogs—they always win. The first day that they kept me indoors I ripped up the couch. But instead of letting me outdoors, they gated off the living room. Next I chewed the red rug, but that didn't work either. They gated off the dining room. The third day I left mawna on the bed, and they gated off the bedroom."

"So they finally put you here?" Bowser asked.

Goldie snorted. "No, the way I got here is when they took me for a run on the beach, I galloped off and chased the wrong bird."

The shed was suddenly alive with discussion of *the wrong bird* as the other dogs, having heard Goldie, joined in. Bowser heard *terrific, outsmarted, half-human,* and *slave.*

All of them were confused by the bird's devoted loyalty to the man. Loyalty was one of a dog's highest virtues, but loyalty in a bird?

"Dog-gone-it, if a bird is going to be loyal, shouldn't she be loyal to a good dog over a bad human?" Handsome whined.

At that point, Toro shifted. The dogs quieted. They watched the big dog get to his feet and stretch his strong front legs, pushing his rear into the air.

"Troops, how long since we've had water and food?" came his loud bark.

For the second time Toro and the others ran through their litany of questions and answers. Bowser joined in the lively responses. He meant to ask Handsome later what Toro meant by 'almost gave his life.'

"Until morning, I'd be grateful for your complete silence, so I can think," Toro finished. "True, our last escape attempt failed because of my hesitation over biting a human. But I am determined to succeed next time. Never doubt it, troops, we shall go free."

Bowser felt his heart pound with excitement. As the dogs leapt up to bark their enthusiasm, he threw himself joyfully into the air and joined their cry: "To freedom. Yea, Master. To freedom!"

Chapter 8

Koko's Australian shepherd grandparents had worked all day on a ranch in Wyoming, moving sheep from pasture to barn and back, and Koko herself ran as fast as she could every chance she got. So, although she'd grown up in the city, she was muscular and strong. Jenny too was a strong dog, though older, and they ran swiftly together, without talking, over the dog path toward Seal Beach. Handsome had been heading toward this beach when he'd vanished, and Koko thought it was a good place to look for clues. The sun had grown hot, and the dogs galloped with their mouths open, panting to cool themselves, as crickets leapt out of their way.

Just before the beach, they stopped for a drink of muddy water under the tall eucalyptus trees in Last Gully. Hearing human voices over the splash of waves, they crept onto the hot sand behind a fallen tree and peered out. Seal Beach stretched north as far as they could see, the green ocean breaking into foamy waves over yellow-gray sand. Up the beach a man and two women stood staring at something on the ground near some beach grass.

"That's Ranger Bill," Koko low-barked.

"Can you see what they're looking at?" Jenny asked.

"No. And the wind's wrong." Koko studied Ranger Bill. He was kneeling to pick something up. Very soon it would be gone, into his pocket or his knapsack or—

Koko took off like a streak, reached the knot of humans, darted among their legs and found the small scene of carnage that gripped them: three tiny broken eggs, and a small dead bird. In Ranger Bill's hand was a collar that Koko could smell right away belonged to Bowser.

"Get that dog out of here," one of the women yelled, and at the same time Ranger Bill hollered, "Scram." Koko sniffed quickly at the broken egg shells and bird, ran into the beach grass, circled wide and dashed back the way she'd come.

"Well done," Jenny barked, as they ascertained that the humans hadn't followed.

"It was Bowser's collar, three broken bird eggs and a killed bird," Koko reported breathlessly.

"Bowser destroyed a nest?"

"That's what they want people to think. But the collar, the eggs, the dead bird—all of them smelled like the van."

Jenny's back fur bristled.

"Plus, the eggs and bird didn't smell anything like Bowser. The dead bird was killed by a falcon."

The dogs peered out again at the trio of humans.

"Ranger Bill will figure out what happened." Koko raised a paw hopefully as she watched him. "He'll get to the bottom of it. He's looking at that collar now. He can probably tell which human touched it and find that human through a machine."

But her paw dropped and her legs stiffened as she watched Ranger Bill stand quietly while the woman who'd yelled at Koko did all the talking. The angry woman flapped her hand over the eggshells, waved it up and down the beach, and finally pointed to where Koko and Jenny hid behind the fallen tree. Ranger Bill didn't appear to be arguing at all. In fact he was slowly nodding.

"He must see that collar couldn't have just fallen off," Koko low-barked. "Bowser just got that new collar."

"If it's a choice between blaming a human or a dog, Ranger Bill usually blames the dog," Jenny growled.

At that point, Ranger Bill, as if he'd heard her, left the other humans and started walking quickly toward the dogs' hiding place. "Let's go," Jenny barked, and the two dogs shot back into Last Gully and set off for home.

Koko ran as fast as before, but a quarter of the way home, Jenny slowed her down. "Lately my legs hurt if I run too much."

Koko glanced at the alpha worriedly. She had met various alphas in her life. Many were like Jenny, calm, sensible and trustworthy, but there were mean alphas too, dogs who scared other dogs into submission. In addition to respecting her, Koko liked Jenny. She didn't want anything happening to her and some hothead breed like a chow taking over.

"I'm worried," Jenny confided, as the two dogs skirted a cow pasture, "that our humans are going to leash us before long. It happened down the coast at Porcupine City."

"I was leashed once," Koko told her, remembering with dismay her old life in the city. Back then she would lie alone around the house or small yard for what seemed like forever, waiting for the sound of Michelle's keys in the door, waiting for Michelle to put on her dirty shoes and her sweatshirt and fetch the leash.

Occasionally Koko had had to wait the entire day. She had seen the light fading from the sky, and Michelle had never come home or sung the Walk Song. Those were hard moments, realizing that they were not going to go out at all. Koko's heart had felt like it was going to break. "But our humans here won't do that to us," she barked to Jenny.

"They might," Jenny replied. "If they do, some Shoretown dogs will be okay. They'll sleep a lot. They'll get heavy. They'll still run, but only in their dreams."

They navigated a narrow place in the path. On one side the cliff fell steeply to the green ocean below.

"If they try to leash me, I'm going to escape and swim out to sea until I can't go any further," Jenny growled suddenly.

Koko stopped short. "No!" She couldn't imagine a dog wanting to die. Giving up on life wasn't a dog-like thing to do. Even an old dog like Jenny.

The alpha trotted on. "Or I might lick up green liquid from the gas station floor, like that young dog did last year. It killed him, and it would kill me even faster."

"But, Jenny," Koko protested, hurrying after her, "you can't kill yourself just because you're leashed. It's not that bad. Lots of dogs are leashed."

"I know, but now you've lived here free, would you want to go back?" Jenny's normally relaxed black and gray tail stiffened.

"Anyway, our humans wouldn't leash us," Koko barked. "They love us."

"So? That just makes it worse." Jenny turned and growled, "If you love a bone, you don't just leave it lying around, do you? You bury it. That's what some of them want to do to us—bury us. Not in the earth like a bone, but in closed rooms and fenced yards and on leashes.

"And," Jenny went on, her bark and hackles rising. "The rest of you dogs aren't helping. No matter how much I warn you about not throwing garbage around when you knock over a can, you're still leaving messes. Humans hate that. Every day at least one of you chases a bird down the beach while a human is watching. They hate that too."

"But—"

Jenny continued, "And now? You saw Ranger Bill. He's going to tell the rest of the humans that Bowser killed a bird."

"But—" Koko protested again, wanting to let Jenny know that Ranger Bill was good at heart, and that everything would be okay, and that Jenny shouldn't think of swimming out to sea nor licking poison.

Jenny's fur was standing on end now, and her lips were drawn back over her teeth as she growled at Koko. "We have problems enough living with humans. And now one of them is out to make us look like slavering wolves."

Koko thought Jenny *did* look like a slavering wolf at the moment, but she didn't say so. Instead, the Aussie looked aside and barked, "If I can find Handsome and Bowser and herd them home, if we can find the gray van and the man that stole them, that will help, won't it?"

Gradually, Jenny's face relaxed, and the fur on her back lay down. "Yes, it will," she barked. "That will help."

Koko followed the alpha's bristled tail. For long moments the Aussie felt panicky at the urgency of her mission and couldn't think at all. But when her mind cleared, she saw in detail her next move.

Chapter 9

When Ranger Bill swung his white truck into the gravel driveway that evening, Koko whimpered. He would be angry that she'd shown up earlier on Seal Beach.

But she wagged her rear end and rushed up to disarm him with her usual leap-and-twirl.

"What in hell were you trying to do at the beach this afternoon?" he asked her, frowning, a chicken-and-garlic-smelling grocery bag in one arm.

Koko leapt way up toward his face, cocking her head and widening her eyes.

"Oh, so you don't know what I'm talking about? You've been here all afternoon at the house, knitting me a sweater?" he chided. He leaned down to ruffle her fur with his free hand.

They banged into the house together. "Michelle, honey, you've got to keep Koko from running off the way she does," he called, as they made their way down the hall into the kitchen. "She was all the way over at Seal Beach this afternoon, giving some birders heart failure."

Michelle appeared at the kitchen door as Bill took the chicken from the grocery bag. Michelle's hair was wet and curly, and she smelled like rosemary bushes. "Was she chasing gulls?"

"No, no, a terrier had killed a snowy plover. She was just having a look-see." As he unwrapped the dead chicken and rinsed it off in the sink, he stuck his hip out. "Reach in my pants pocket."

Smiling, Michelle did as he said, and pulled out Bowser's new collar, tan-colored and embroidered with red bones. Her smile faded. "What's this?"

"There's your villain," Ranger Bill said. "Bowser. You know him?"

"Of course I know him. He's Daisy's wheaten terrier puppy."

"Yes. Well, I just talked to Daisy. Bowser's been gone since this morning. Snapped at her and ran off. She has no idea where he is.

"I read her the riot act about keeping him more under control," Ranger Bill continued. "She can't, she said. He doesn't pay any attention to her. She's at her wits' end, but can't give him up. He's basically sweet, she said."

Ranger Bill took six flaky heads of garlic out of the shopping bag and stuffed them into the chicken. "Trouble is, that woman is too soft to deal with a bad dog."

Michelle fingered the collar. "This was at Seal Beach?"

"Yeah, unfastened like that. He didn't slip it." He took a metal pan with a rack out of a cupboard and laid the wrinkled white chicken on it.

Although normally all of Koko's attention would have been on the plucked bird, she jumped up, her front paws against Michelle's thighs, to sniff Bowser's collar and look at Michelle meaningfully. *Smell it*, she barked, *smell it. Bowser's been stolen by a bad man in a van. You can tell from the smell.*

But humans never smelled things like dog collars. "Yes, it's your friend, Bowser's," Michelle told her. She turned to Bill. "It seems strange that a new collar like this would fall off just as Bowser was up to mischief. It must not have been fastened. But if so, why didn't it fall off before? Seal Beach is a good thirty minute run for a dog."

"You got me." Ranger Bill took a couple of yams out of his grocery bag, rinsed them briefly, poked a fork into each and set them on the rack beside the chicken. Then he thrust the pan into the oven and turned it on. "There, dinner will be ready in an hour and ten minutes." He took a package of frozen peas from his paper bag and, tearing the wrapping off, stuck the green slab into a saucepan, added a little water and stuck the pan on top of a burner. "Chicken, cranberry sauce, yams and peas. How's that sound?" He plunked a small can of cranberry sauce onto the counter with a flourish.

"Great. You make first-rate dinners, honey," Michelle told him in the same encouraging tone she regularly used when he cooked. Ranger Bill always made the same thing: garlic chicken. Sometimes he baked white potatoes instead of yams, and sometimes he cooked frozen corn instead of peas, but Koko couldn't remember him ever making anything but garlic chicken.

"It's not right—Koko ranging all over like she does," he said as he took a pitcher of iced tea from the fridge and poured two glasses. "There're cars, there're traps, there're crazy people."

"Koko's okay," Michelle said, examining Bowser's collar again with a frown. "She can handle herself."

"Bowser had eaten most of a plover and destroyed two eggs. I had to promise those birders I'd put a temporary dog close on Seal Beach tomorrow morning. You think if Koko runs over there again she's going to be able to read a sign saying *No dogs allowed* and turn around and run back home? I know she's smart. But not that smart."

"Oh, Bill," Michelle said, and Koko sensed her frustration. "Why can't those birders leave us alone?"

"At least think about keeping her home this month while the plovers are nesting. I'd be glad to put a fence up, give her a big yard to play in. You'd like that, wouldn't you, Kokomo?"

Hearing his nickname for her, Koko wagged her rear end.

"How can you think she'd like that?" Michelle protested. Ranger Bill had left the bloody chicken wrapping in the sink. Michelle picked it up, rinsed it and thrust it in the trash, then squirted her hands with soap. "She loves being free to come and go when she wants, to see her friends, to race down the beach after a bird."

Sensing Michelle was upset, Koko trotted to her and jumped up, trying to reach Michelle's face. Michelle knelt and hugged Koko so hard it hurt. Koko eased her head around to lick Michelle's hot cheek.

"*Race after a bird*—you said it yourself, Michelle. Birds have enough problems finding food to eat these days without having to deal with dogs chasing them."

Then Ranger Bill added in a defensive tone, "And I would have washed off that chicken wrapping. I just hadn't gotten around to it."

"Dogs are part of the natural world. They have just as much right to it as birds." Michelle rinsed the sink with a brush, cleanser and steaming water from the tap.

Ranger Bill sighed and went over to hug her from behind. "Maybe once, honey, but we've given dogs as much of an advantage in Shoretown as we humans have. Dogs aren't part of nature any more than we are. We feed them, house them, breed them, forgive them their sins. Birds are a different story. They're natural and wild. If they don't find food, they die."

Michelle, smelling angry, extracted herself from his embrace to dry her hands and open the kitchen door. A cool breeze with whiffs of skunk and night heron blew in. She stood looking out at the pines and scrub. "I don't care. I may be a monster, but I don't care. I am not locking Koko up. If she gets hurt or killed, I'll deal with it. It'll be horrible, but we'll get through it. I am not locking her up. If they pass that leash law Friday, and those blockheads tell me I have to keep her fenced or leashed, I'll up and move."

Ranger Bill smelled suddenly anxious as he watched Michelle's stiff back. "Come on, honey, don't talk like that."

Michelle closed the door again and stood, drumming her fingers on the counter. "It kills me. Half the sympathetic people I've been phoning these last few days are with us, but the others hem and haw. One of them says she loves dogs, but she's realized after watching some TV show that birds are the last wild symbol of the spirit. How's she going to react when she hears Bowser killed a snowy plover?"

Michelle sat down at the table and stood up again restlessly.

Ranger Bill opened his mouth to speak, but Michelle continued, "That doped-up guy Ed who hangs out near the bakery believes that dogs like Handsome are going to turn wild and form packs. He saw it in a vision, he said. He said dogs from all over the area are vanishing. There are two missing from Porcupine City, he said. In his vision he saw ten dogs meeting in the woods howling like wolves. You can bet he'll be spreading that story all over town."

"Nobody in their right mind listens to Ed's visions." Bill drained his glass and set it in the sink.

"But there is no *right mind* in this town. Ed said there was a pack of dogs that went wild years ago, and these dogs are their natural descendents. You know how some people in this town, when they hear the word *natural,* roll over on their backs and buy anything."

"They're probably the same ones who'd stick up for dogs going wild. They'd still vote against the leash law."

Michelle brightened. "I hadn't thought of that." She picked up the empty grocery bag and folded it absently. "But dogs going missing . . . I don't like that at all. Especially Handsome." She looked at Koko, who, upon hearing Handsome's name, had jumped up eagerly. "You're sweet on him, aren't you, honey?"

"If they're not confined, country dogs will take off sometimes, Michelle," Ranger Bill said. "It's in their blood."

"But why are they taking off right now? I don't get it. Something's wrong."

Michelle smelled different suddenly. Koko eyed her human and sniffed.

There was something in Michelle that reminded Koko of a baying hound. Koko's ears came forward, and she leaned forward on her toes.

Michelle had begun to hunt!

"There's no telling when and why dogs will suddenly go wild, honey." Ranger Bill stood up and walked over to Michelle. He seemed to grow taller as he pulled her into his arms. As they kissed, Michelle's hunting smell faded and disappeared.

Koko slumped back with half-closed eyes. Ranger Bill should be bitten on the leg. If he didn't leave Michelle alone, Koko would hold him personally responsible for whatever bad things happened next.

Chapter 10

After Michelle's bedroom grew quiet that night, Koko rose from her spot on the living room floor and stretched carefully, first her front legs and chest, then each back leg. It worried her that she'd be leaving Michelle. It was her hereditary duty to guard Michelle through the night. But since Ranger Bill was in bed next to her, and he was something like a guard dog himself, it was probably okay. Now, for instance, as Koko made her way into the kitchen and took a long drink of water, she could sense him waking and turning over in bed. He was a light sleeper like her.

She flipped through her dog door, which banged behind her no matter how slowly she moved, and sniffed around for a good place to relieve herself. Any place would do for a pee, but for your mawna you needed just the right feel. You knew the spot when you found it. Here was a good one. Koko squatted and worked her muscles, lowering her eyelids pleasurably at the satisfying elimination of mawna.

It would be better if Ranger Bill, and Michelle, if she happened to wake, heard the dog door bang again. They would feel safe, thinking her back in the house. Koko trotted back to the door, started in, then backed out again. The dog door banged shut.

On Pine Street, moonlight fluttered through the tree leaves and shone on the roofs of the houses. Koko knew to avoid Roggie's house. As a sensitive Sheltie, Roggie was compelled to bark at anything unusual like a dog prowling late at night.

Skunks were out. The Aussie slowed, seeing a mother and two little ones waddling across the dirt road in front of her. They were after the greens near the water plant. It was stupid to chase a skunk, but normally she would have. They sensed her and sped up, their white-striped tails disappearing into the brush.

Turning onto the path to Seal Beach, Koko picked up her pace. This was when she was happiest, running as fast as she could, taking the curves as they came.

She knew Handsome felt the same. His exuberant nature came out in that graceful reach and pull of his long powerful legs. Sweet Handsome, Koko thought, where are you?

A raccoon was washing something in the little pool of muddy water at Last Gully, and Koko barked at it to move. The raccoon turned. It was a big animal with an arrogant air, but the Aussie bristled out her fur, bared her teeth and barked again. The raccoon dipped its bit of food one more time in the water and retreated.

Koko sniffed the edge of the dark pond. Her nose picked up Bowser's scent amongst others. She followed Bowser's track out onto the moonlit sand and immediately lost it. She stood slightly forward, her ears pricked, eyes wide. The strip of beach stretched out before her, ocean on one side, sea grasses, low dunes and woods on the other.

Before Bowser was stolen, the van must have crossed from the woods to the beach, or Bowser must have crossed from the beach to the woods. So if Koko sniffed along the edge of the grasses, she must eventually pick up the scent of either the puppy or the van.

She loped along the grasses, her nose to the ground. The sand was silvery bright in the moonlight. Above her she sensed the starry sky and nearby the huge noisy ocean—*ka-splash, ka-splash.*

Abruptly, she stopped. Yes, there it was: faint, but definitely Bowser. The purple-black grasses must have brushed against him as he ran. Her nose quivering, Koko followed his trail over the dunes and down a narrow path toward the woods.

Suddenly, she smelled the van. Koko flattened her ears and raised her hackles as she crept through the twisted junipers and oaks, the smell of the van growing stronger.

This was it! This was where Bowser had been stolen. Koko raised her nose, cleared it by breathing fresh air, then bent to sniff again. Yes, definitely. Bowser's scent ended right here. Nearby were bent branches and tire tracks and Koko could smell oil from the van, rubber tires and the man's shoes.

Over each strong scent, Koko rolled her furry body, waving her legs in the air so the twisting movement would cement the smells. She sniffed the trunk of a tree the man must have crouched against and rubbed her shoulder on the bark where his back must have rested.

The man's trail led into the woods and she followed, at first tentatively, then with determination, leaping over fallen trees and plunging through thorny bushes and beds of ferns. After a while, his trail led out into the grasses.

Koko's fur bristled as she came upon two downy gray feathers and some hardened drops of bird blood on the sand. This was where the snowy plover had been killed by the man's falcon. The Aussie growled low.

A lone cloud passed over the bright moon, and Koko felt its shadow fall over her. She continued tracking the man through the dunes and grasses and soon came out onto the beach at the exact spot where the broken shells and dead bird had been that afternoon. They were gone now.

The Aussie looked down the beach toward the fallen tree where she and Jenny had hidden. This afternoon they had sensed that something was badly wrong, and they'd been right.

Koko sank to the sand. There was no doubt now of the bad man's guilt. There was a chance she and the other dogs could hunt him down before he did something terrible to Handsome and Bowser. But it would be hard without human help.

Koko whimpered. Far from helping, Ranger Bill and other humans seemed to believe that their dogs were going bad.

Except for Michelle, Koko thought. She must try to get through to Michelle. The Aussie jumped up and moved to the spot where Bowser's collar had been found. There she sat, tilted her head back and howled her determination at the moon.

Chapter 11

Over the roar of the waterfall and the panting and scratching of dogs, Bowser woke to hear sparrow chitter. Light sliced through a chink in the boards, but generally the shed was dark. It was the morning of the puppy's second day of captivity. During the night he'd been waked up by a scuffle in one dark corner. 'Stupid' had bitten 'Dumbhead' for encroaching onto his spot. Toro had intervened. There'd been a thud and then silence.

Bowser's mouth felt like it was full of parched sand. His stomach growled. Fleas had colonized him during the night, and their bites burned and itched. His muscles ached as he stretched.

He had been waked a second time in the night by an announcement from Toro. "I am working on my grand plan of escape. Please maintain complete silence." Bowser had just been able to make out the big alpha sitting tall near the door, a powerful force in the darkness.

Goldie had asked sleepily, "What is this grand plan, Master?"

"I'll tell it to you in the morning when your minds are clear."

A little later Toro had low-barked his plan to Bowser. At least he must have, for Bowser had waked knowing it.

Handsome's black paw touched Bowser as the Lab stretched his strong legs and flexed his shoulders. Goldie was relieving herself in the privy corner, as was one of the mutts.

But it was Toro whom Bowser stared at. The big dog lay unmoving in his spot with his eyes open. "Why is Toro like that?" Bowser asked Handsome.

Handsome padded over and stretched his black nose toward Toro. "Master?" he whimpered.

When nothing happened Bowser and the other dogs crowded around. Indeed Toro seemed to have lost his electricity, like a switched-off TV. He lay on his side, his great strong body limp, his eyes open but looking nowhere.

Goldie finally ventured, "Excuse me, Master, but what about your grand plan of escape?"

Toro was silent. His eyes remained blank.

The dogs stirred uneasily at this behavior in their alpha.

Bowser turned toward Handsome, threw himself on his small back, and looked away, for, in the absence of Toro's leadership, Handsome seemed like a natural choice for alpha, mature and strong as he was.

But Handsome promptly rolled over on his own back!

The two dogs who'd fought during the night were goading each other. "Greed-Paw," one taunted, and the other growled, "Hang-Tail." Their lips curled, and their ears folded back. Other dogs anxiously clicked their teeth at fleas. Goldie was trying to bite her own tail, and the trembling hound had started barking incessantly in a pitiful voice.

Bowser yelped in dismay. Very soon the shed would be full of frenzied dogs. And Toro was still lying inert.

The puppy raised his hackles, pricked forward his small ears and barked sharply three times. "Master has come up with a grand plan of escape."

At this, the room quieted. The dogs' eyes moved back and forth between Bowser and Toro, who raised his head to stare at the pup.

"Master told me his grand plan of escape during the night," Bowser barked. "Master has decreed we will dig a tunnel."

"A tunnel!" Toro snarled in derision and lay down again.

The other dogs whined in dismay. "The walls and floor are too thick," the shepherd whimpered.

Bowser went on quickly, "That was true before, but Master has realized that in the area of the privy, where pee and mawna have soaked the floor for days, the floorboards are rotting. They're like old sticks in a pond. Master believes—"

But he was cut off by Toro who suddenly stood up to loom over the others and dominate the shed again. His deep bark rumbled out. "I believe we should break through those soft floorboards and tunnel our way to freedom."

There were spontaneous barks of enthusiasm. Dogs jumped with joy. "To Master's grand escape plan. To freedom!"

"O Master, when do you think we should start on your great tunnel to freedom?" Goldie whimpered.

"Immediately. There is no time to waste," Toro barked. "We shall divide into teams. When the time comes to use our teeth, I will do much of the work but for this first phase I will be the manager."

Bowser was assigned to the first team with Handsome and Goldie. Together they waded into the privy corner, trying to avoid the piles of mawna. "Here's a crack between the floorboards, Master," Handsome pointed out. "Shall we start to dig here?"

"Certainly. That looks like the best spot," Toro agreed.

"Bowser, you're a genius," Goldie low-barked, as the three began to scratch at the damp wood with their claws.

Bowser liked the sound of that. "I am?" He winced as a splinter entered his paw. The boards were slippery with pee and mawna, and the flies were especially thick. "You mean yelling out Master's plan?"

"That wasn't *his* plan. He never thinks of digging—it's not something he likes to do. That was your plan."

"Mine?" Bowser stopped digging to contemplate his own brilliance.

"Keep digging there, Pup," Toro reminded him.

"Yes, Master." Bowser bent to his work again. Not Toro's plan, but his own? Shouldn't he be getting some of the credit then, sitting managing things at Toro's side rather than wrecking his paws here in this sea of mawna?

"It was very noble of you, pretending your plan was his," Goldie went on. "The Great Bahoo once did a similar thing in his youth, so they say. He helped his alpha out of a fix by taking the blame for a bad decision. Don't expect any public credit, Bowser. We'll all act as though it was Master who saved us and not you."

Handsome barked, "Who cares who gets the credit anyway? What does it matter?"

Goldie looked puzzled. "Ah, but you're a strange animal, Handsome. Any other dog with your strength and good nature would have taken over from Toro this morning. Why didn't you? We all would have followed you."

Handsome glanced at her. "Just because I'm big and black everyone thinks I want to lead. Dog-gone-it, I'm no alpha. I don't want to boss other dogs around. I don't want them idolizing me, and I don't want them hating me."

Bowser was confused at Handsome's modesty. Handsome was one of the most likable dogs around, and yet he was admitting to such weakness. How could any dog not want to be alpha?

To avoid dwelling on Handsome's faults, the terrier asked, "Tell me about when Master tried to lead an escape."

Goldie shifted her stance slightly to attack the floor from a different angle. "It happened when the man brought Handsome in."

Handsome wagged his otter tail. "That's right," he barked cheerfully.

Goldie continued, "You probably saw, Bowser, that there's a fenced yard outside this shed. The man used to leave the gate to that yard unlocked when he brought a new dog in. So a few days ago Toro told us that the next time the man opened the door, he would lunge at him and knock him over. Then we'd all gallop out the door, dash through the open gate and escape into the woods."

Bowser stopped digging and opened his mouth in anticipation, letting his pink tongue hang out.

"When the man opened the door to thrust Handsome in, Toro attacked. But something went wrong, and the man didn't fall over. Instead he reached out to grab Toro by the back leg and throw him down. Toro struggled, but he couldn't free himself."

"Toro could have bitten the man's hand," Handsome put in, "but he didn't."

Bowser's ears flattened, and his heart thumped with excitement. "If he had bitten the man, Toro might have been shot." Every dog knew that biting a human could carry a sentence of death.

"Yes," Goldie agreed, "but the reason Toro's been so strange these last few days is that he's blamed himself for *not* biting that man. Toro was my alpha at Porcupine City, and I've never seen him as loco as he is here. He barks the bark, but he's really running around like a chicken with its head cut off by a farmer. The man keeps the gate locked now, and Toro hasn't been able to come up with another plan. But you've given him one, Bowser, and he's back to his old self. I'll never forget you for that."

Bowser beamed at the compliment and went at the work furiously. Soon his paws were hurting badly, he felt splinters lodged under his nails, and his white feet and legs and pink belly were stained brown and yellow. It was nice to have Goldie's admiration but maybe the other dogs had been right—these boards were too thick to pierce.

"Troops," Toro suddenly barked, "how long since we've had water and food?"

"Three days," the dogs chorused.

"How long since we've been allowed in the yard?"

"Three days!"

"What's the longest any dog's been here?"

"Nineteen days!"

"Will our humans save us?"

"No!"

"Are we giving up?"

"No!" the dogs barked, stronger now.

"Who's going to lead you out of here?"

"You, Master!"

"Who almost gave his life to set you free?"

"You, Master!"

"Who's come up with a perfect plan of escape?"

"You, Master!" the dogs howled.

Toro's big tail thumped against the floor. "Team One," he barked. "Time to rest. Team Two, it's your turn."

As they returned to the cleaner part of the shed Bowser cast a glance at what they'd accomplished. Not too much. There were some deep gouges on the floor, and the mawna was smeared around, but the deeper they'd dug in the floor, the harder and dryer and stronger the wood had become.

Yet the three dogs of the second team were applying themselves with gusto, their heads close together, their claws scraping the wood vigorously, almost as if they were digging cool holes in the beach sand. The beach sand, yes . . . with the refreshing spray of the ocean and the big blue sky. Bowser dozed off.

Chapter 12

Piccolo was determined to make Koko respect him. For one thing, he admired her proud stance. There she stood beside Jenny at Bushy Corner, her Aussie body sturdy and graceful, the reddish fur on her head and back thick and fluffy, her white muzzle freckled, her strong white-furred legs dotted with an occasional stick or seed. Second, there was the matter of his own pride. His kind, what humans called Jack Russell terriers, were a proud race and it was embarrassing to think Koko might think, because of that stupid remark he'd made about smelling cigarette smoke downtown, that he was a dunderhead.

"Last night Koko found the spot where Bowser was captured and stuck in the van," Jenny told the dogs at Bushy Corner. "She rolled in the smells there. So now I want everyone to line up and rub against her fur so you'll all know what the van smells like and exactly what we're looking for."

Piccolo sniffed the breeze from Koko's direction. Yes, he could smell a great stew of scents.

Koko was what they all called a city dog. Piccolo tried to picture the city. All he knew was that most of the dogs there were educated. Piccolo pictured them sitting on chairs at the schoolhouse like the children of Shoretown staring at a colored picture of a dog.

"Rosa," he asked, for immediately ahead of him in line was Rosa's sleek Springer spaniel body with its short tail. "When a dog goes to class in the city, does a dog or a human teach the class?"

"A human, silly," Rosa snapped, turning to give him a supercilious look.

Piccolo drew himself up. "Have you been to one?"

"I wouldn't deign to go," Rosa answered.

"Don't you want to expand your knowledge?" he barked.

"I know all I want to know," Rosa said. It was her turn, and Piccolo watched as, short tail erect, she stalked up to Koko, rubbed her shoulder against Koko's a few times, and then stalked off.

Piccolo glanced at Jenny to see if she'd reproach Rosa for her bad manners, but the alpha just low-barked something to Koko and nodded to Piccolo to come up next.

Piccolo had planned to say something insightful and delightful to Koko, but he was struck dumb as he walked up to her. What a magnificent animal! She seemed to vibrate with life. He could see she was tired. The corners of her eyes were red. His urge was to sniff her, but Jenny had emphasized there wasn't time. Koko had to get home to work. A quick rub against her body was all he could dare.

That was another way in which Koko was exotic. She had a real job. She was expected to be at work at nine in the morning and stay until noon. Piccolo wasn't sure what she did, but it had something to do with sitting in a room with humans, listening intently to their gibberish and comforting them if they felt bad. Maybe she licked them. Although, in his experience, most humans didn't care to be licked.

Piccolo stood looking up at Koko. No matter how tall he tried to stand on his small feet, he wasn't tall enough. Koko gave him a friendly look and lowered herself so he could rub against her. She was like a goddess stepping to earth. She was big and firm and furry. This was like heaven. He could have stayed there for ages, but Jenny barked for him to move on.

As he trotted back home to make sure his humans were okay and see if they'd planned anything special for today, Piccolo turned to sniff his side. Now he smelled like her. But also he detected a particular variety of car oil, a singed rubber smell and an unfamiliar male human. How impressed Koko would be when he, Piccolo, caught the bad man. He sniffed a stand of coyote bush at the side of Pine Street. No, he'd stake his life on it: the man had not been hiding in this particular spot. He moved on with a serious air, pausing to examine various bushes.

By the time he arrived home, his humans had left for their jobs at the grocery store. He'd delayed too long. If he wanted to go downtown to lie on the grocery store porch, he'd have to walk.

He went to his outdoor water dish, a shiny metal bowl, and looked into it. An orange ladybug was struggling in the water near a brown leaf. She was trying to swim to the leaf. Unfortunately her movements seemed to drive the leaf farther away. Piccolo thought she must be tiring and getting discouraged. With his nose he tipped the bowl over. The water quickly sank into the ground. He looked for the ladybug. She had landed on her back and was now trying to right herself by waving her legs. What a life, being a bug. Piccolo was glad he was a dog, even a small dog.

He sat eagerly by the side of the road, waiting to see if the van came along. Time passed, and the only person to go by was a girl on a bicycle. The sun grew hotter, and he grew thirstier. Downtown there'd be more cars and people. Plus his humans always put a bowl of water out on the grocery store porch.

Which reminded him, he was supposed to be on duty on the porch, watching for the van. Piccolo yelped.

The little terrier ran to the middle of Elm Street and headed downtown.

Shortly he felt a vehicle come up behind him. He turned and looked at it suspiciously. No, it was not a van but a dirty white car. It honked at him and he shifted a little to the left. It honked again, and he sped up a little. What did it want?

The car came up alongside him very slowly, almost grazing his right side. Piccolo considered lunging at its tire, but decided against it. Instead he chased it to Main Street, barking.

Downtown smelled familiar. Many bushes and trees were flowering. Pockets of sweet were mixed in with the usual human and car and food scents. Someone had dropped part of a sticky bun in a gutter, and Piccolo gulped it down. He climbed up to the grocery store porch and had a drink of water as chaser. Then he pushed open the screen door, trotted behind the counter and looked up into each of his humans' faces. His male human said, "Out, Piccolo," and his female human said the same thing. Piccolo rolled over, spun around, sighed and left.

He stood on the porch outside the store and looked both ways. No strange vans. Bucky and Ruby came up the stairs to sniff him. The two old yellow dogs lived behind the store in the yard of an old house. They were never allowed indoors, which was too bad. On the other hand, they never had to have a bath or go to the vet. Ruby had had something wrong with one of her back legs for years. She held it up off the ground most of the time.

"Howdy," Piccolo said.

"Howdy," they barked back, settling down nearby to scratch fleas.

Piccolo again looked both ways. Across the street was the bakery with its delicious treats, but he would probably not be allowed in. Toward the ocean to the right was the hardware store that sold boring dog food and handed out boring biscuits.

While he was wondering which store to head for, the terrier kept one eye fixed on the road coming into town. When a strange van appeared, Piccolo saw it immediately. The van was old, blue and battered, and it came straight down the street and parked almost in front of him. A young human male stepped out and came up the stairs to the porch. Piccolo stood in his way in fighting position, his back legs like steel, his front legs braced forward, his eyes blazing.

"Move over, little guy," the young man said. Piccolo could smell the man was a little afraid. Well, no wonder, Piccolo thought. This man had taken Bowser and Handsome and was about to be found out. The man moved to the side, and Piccolo shifted like lightning to stop him from entering the store. Strange van, strange man—this must be him. He didn't smell like any of the smells Piccolo was after, but that was okay. He must be in disguise. He had even changed the color of his van. Clever man, but not clever enough for Piccolo. Koko and Jenny would be so impressed. Piccolo curled his lip and snarled.

"Hey," the man called into the store. "Does this dog belong to someone in there?"

Almost immediately, Piccolo's human female pushed the swinging screen door open. "Piccolo," she said in her sternest tone. "Stop it this instant."

Piccolo ceased snarling and took a step aside. He growled as the man edged carefully past him to the door.

"He wouldn't hurt you," Piccolo's female human said.

"He does a good imitation," the man said. He assumed a friendly air, although Piccolo could sense from his voice he was up to no good. "Great store."

Piccolo's humans said something back.

"How long've you had it?" the man asked.

Piccolo stood watching intently through the screen door while the humans talked on and on. Another customer came and went, forcing Piccolo to move twice.

Finally, when the sun had moved onto the deck and was burning down on Piccolo's back half, the strange man started out again. As he swung open the screen door, Piccolo lunged at his leg. His little teeth went straight through the man's pants and sock and touched flesh. The man yelled, "Hey," and kicked out. Piccolo was thrown off the porch and landed on the pavement next to a parked car.

"Wha—" Piccolo's humans had come to the door.

"Your dog bit me," the man cried.

Piccolo struggled to his feet and staggered onto the sidewalk and up the few stairs back onto the porch. Again he rushed at the man, who was crouched down, his pant leg pulled up, examining his hairy leg.

"Piccolo," his male human said angrily, reaching down and grabbing him under the belly. "What's got into you?"

Piccolo was held helpless against his human's khaki shirt. At first he barked at the bad man from his ignominious position, but his human put a stop to that by holding his jaw closed so his barks came out muffled.

"It's okay. It didn't break the skin," the man said, pushing down his pant leg and standing up.

"Here, let me get you something," Piccolo's human said to the man, and still keeping Piccolo in his vet-type grip, went into the store, picked up half a dozen Clif bars, and, returning outside, held them out. "Take 'em," he said. "I'm sorry about the dog."

Piccolo tried to bark louder. His human was actually giving delicious food to the bad man. It was inconceivable.

"Thanks," the stranger said, reaching out while keeping an eye on Piccolo, who was glaring at him from behind his human's hand. "Tough little character. I hope he's not hurt. I kicked out and over he went."

"Aww, he's fine."

Just then Jenny came trotting up. Piccolo sent her messages with his eyes, rolling them toward the van and the man. Jenny glanced at the van, wrinkled her nose a little toward the man and continued on her way.

Piccolo thought hard. How come Jenny wasn't doing anything? Now he remembered that he was supposed to pee hard on the tires of the van if he saw it, so later the dogs could follow its trail. How come Jenny wasn't doing that, seeing he was out of commission? Perhaps she figured he had already done it. But he hadn't. He'd forgotten.

Now the stranger was getting into the van. He was starting the engine. He was backing out and leaving the way he'd come. He'd be passing right by Jenny. Perhaps she would lunge out and do something as he drove by. But no, the van had passed her. Jenny was doing nothing!

Wriggling back against his human's body as hard as he could, Piccolo managed to squirm out of his arms, land in a heap on the porch, right himself and go racing past Jenny and after the van, barking. "It's him, Jenny, it's him."

"It is *not* him, Piccolo. It doesn't smell anything like him."

"In disguise," Piccolo barked back breathlessly as he raced.

"No, Piccolo."

Not him? Piccolo couldn't believe it. Of course it was him. But Jenny had said no, and Jenny knew everything. On Piccolo raced, the van speeding up and leaving him behind as it left town. He could just make out the squiggles on the license plate. Now, just the shape of the van. In the next moment it disappeared around a curve and was gone.

He stopped and sat, panting, by the side of the road, looking at the spot where the van had vanished.

Not him? After all this? Piccolo's brain couldn't take it in. But Jenny had barked those words: "Not him," and Jenny was never wrong.

Piccolo crept under a nearby bush to lie down and whimper. He was thirsty. If he hid here long enough, he might die of thirst. Then everyone would be sorry. His humans would be sorry they got angry at him, and all the dogs in town would be sorry they'd scorned him for chasing the wrong man. They were probably already pant-laughing and yodeling at his expense. "Oh, that Piccolo," they'd be saying, "such a character. Absolutely determined and yet he got the *wrong man.*"

Piccolo lay with his tail between his legs. Nobody cares, he thought. He was thirsty, but so what? Who cared? No one apparently. Occasionally the tires of a car would go by a few yards away, but so what if he got run over? At least he wouldn't have to go through the embarrassment of seeing Koko amused by his mistake or hearing Jenny growl at him that he had failed.

Piccolo closed his eyes and was soon asleep.

He woke up to someone poking him with her nose. "Wake up, Piccolo," Jenny said.

He rolled onto his back and looked submissively away from her wide gray and black face. "I'm sorry, Jenny." Small cones and sticks poked him in the back, but he hardly noticed.

"That's all right. Everyone makes mistakes," Jenny said. "But I want you to tell me again what I said this morning about finding the man who took Bowser and Handsome."

"He and the van will smell like Koko did this morning," Piccolo recited.

"Did that man today smell like that? Or his van?"

"No. But I thought he was in disguise."

"There's no reason he'd be in disguise. He doesn't know we're looking for him."

Piccolo thought about this. He stood up and wagged his tail, then nudged Jenny with his muzzle. "I didn't think of that."

Jenny licked him back. "You may still find the right man, Piccolo. If you do, what are you supposed to do?"

"Pee on the tires so we can follow his trail."

"Did you do that with this van?"

"I forgot."

"That's just as well. And if you do find the man, don't let him know you know. No barking, biting, and so forth. Understood?"

Piccolo blinked in agreement. "Understood."

"Now I think you have an excellent chance of finding this man since you can spend a good part of the day at the grocery store. If your humans don't tie you up, that is."

"So I'm still on the case?" Piccolo asked hopefully. He would worry about being tied up later.

"Of course," and Jenny trotted off.

Chapter 13

All morning the dogs worked on their hole in the floor of the shed, their shoulders hunched, the collar boxes poking their throats. It was Bowser's eighth turn. His paws stung and throbbed as he scratched the hard wood.

Handsome and Goldie clawed with the grain of the wood, Bowser across it. Every so often, when a long splinter came loose, the dogs yipped in celebration.

Although occasionally one of them yelped in pain, even Goldie's previously sad eyes were hopeful. What had before been simply a knot of gouges was now a wide depression in the floor.

Bowser thought he might black out with thirst. It was torture, having to listen to the rushing waterfall outside and not having a drop in here. He glanced at the other dogs. Everyone's paws were bloody. How, when their paws were already bleeding from wood splinters, were they ever going to finish this hole through the floor, much less dig an escape tunnel through the dirt under the shed?

"Soon we can use our teeth," Toro barked, as if he'd read the puppy's mind.

At the same moment, all the dogs raised their heads. On the wisps of air seeping in under the door and around the boards of the windows came the cigarette smell of the man and faint whiffs of kibble.

"Food," Handsome barked. The other dogs joined him in jumping up and down, battering the door with their paws.

"Silence," Toro barked.

They quieted.

"We must protect our hole," Toro said. "The bad man's coming to give us food and water. He'll have his bird play with us, and some of us will feel the terrible pain. But always, when he feeds us, he also cleans out the shed, shoveling out our mawna and rinsing the floor off. When he sees that we're digging a hole, he'll plug it up."

The dogs looked at the bloodstained shallow pit in dismay.

"I could hide it like this," Handsome suggested, lying down on top of the hole, ignoring the mawna on all sides.

"He's going to want to shovel out that mawna. He'll make you move," Toro pointed out.

The man's scent grew stronger. They could hear his footsteps on the path and his voice talking to his bird. He was fiddling with the clasp of the gate into the yard.

"We'll have to move the mawna," Goldie said.

"Quickly," the alpha agreed. "He won't take long setting up our food and water."

Although the dogs did not like touching their mawna, they all, including Toro, began to clear it from around the hole. Each of them squatted and hurled piles of it back between their hind legs against the far wall, where it slid to the floor. By the time the man could be heard relocking the gate, most of the mawna had been moved to the far wall. Each dog had done his or her best to pee there too.

"Okay," Toro told them. Handsome settled himself over the hole, while the rest of them barked excitedly and jumped against the door.

"All right, keep your pants on," the man said, as he undid the lock to the shed. The door opened, the man pulled it wide and the dogs dashed out into the yard in an explosion of fur and barking.

A human! Even if he was a bad one. Bowser jumped up to try to lick the man's face. Then, seeing the other dogs race to a big dishpan full of water, he followed and thrust his muzzle in, drinking eagerly.

When it was empty, the dogs turned toward two standing pails of water, but the man shooed them toward the large bowl of food. Even though, as a pup, he had to wait to eat, Bowser kept his eyes fastened firmly on the food. Finally, the scrawny hound ahead of him was pushed aside with a foot. The man poured out more kibble, Bowser took his place at the bowl, took a mouthful of pellets, greedily swallowed them whole, and was reaching for a second bite when he felt Toro at his shoulder. "Bowser, relieve Handsome. He needs to eat."

"Wha—?"

"Into the shed and lie on the hole. Pronto."

It was so unfair, Bowser thought, as he left the sunshine and trees behind and trudged back inside to take Handsome's place. As Handsome vanished out the door, Bowser sank down over the hole and lay his chin flat on the floor. He could hear the other dogs gobbling kibble. And he'd had only one mouthful. So what if Daisy had given him part of a hamburger yesterday morning, while the others hadn't eaten for three days. That didn't mean he wasn't starving now. Bowser flopped to his side.

The man tromped into the shed with a shovel, and Bowser raised his head to look at him.

"You like it here in this stink, do you?" the man said, as he slid the shovel under a big pile of Toro mawna and carried it back outside.

Back and forth the man went, cleaning off the floor of the shed. Finally he returned with a pail of water and threw it over the area he'd just cleaned. Some of the water sluiced over to where Bowser lay. Bowser reached out a tongue to taste it, then spit it out.

The man came back with another pail of water. "Okay, better move." Bowser didn't understand the words, but he heard the warning in them and saw that the man was

66

about to throw the water his way. "Okay, if that's the way you want it." The man threw the cold water right over Bowser. What a delicious shock. The water puddled around for a second and then ran down toward the hole under Bowser.

But the man didn't notice. "You're going to have to come out for class. I didn't buy those fancy training collars so you could lie around here sleeping. Come on." Bowser didn't move. The man took a few steps toward him, reached down, grabbed his collar, and started to drag him.

"He's dragging me off the hole. Do something!" the puppy barked. Immediately, the other dogs growled and snarled furiously, as if they were tearing a bird to shreds. As the man looked back toward them in alarm, Bowser jumped to his feet and headed to the door.

"It worked. He didn't notice," Bowser low-barked to the others. He went straight to the food dish and filled himself up. Sensing someone watching, he looked up to see the falcon staring at him from the branch of a nearby tree. *Ha,* Bowser barked at her, *you think you're so smart, but we dogs are smarter.*

The man had locked the gate and was squatting now outside the fence, fiddling with a black box. "Okay," he said finally. "This'll teach you mutts." He fetched the bird and carried her to the far side of the fence, placing her on a low tree branch there. Then he returned to his black box and made a motion with his chin to the bird. At once the bird flew in a leisurely way across the fenced-in dogs, dipping low to tease them. As the dogs raced around excitedly, Bowser leapt up to chomp at the bird, who easily dodged him.

Goldie yelped and cowered in pain.

"Damn," the man muttered. "What's wrong with this thing?"

The dogs gathered around the golden. "Was it the terrible pain?" Handsome asked.

Goldie didn't answer, just whimpered and breathed raggedly.

"Are you still feeling it?" Toro asked.

Goldie looked up. "No, I'm all right." But Bowser thought a light had gone out of her amber eyes, and bitterness had returned.

Until the terrible pain happened to him, Bowser enjoyed the class. Sure, he felt awfully sorry for the dogs like Goldie who suddenly yelped and cringed. But after a short time the hurt dogs seemed almost back to normal, just a little fearful, and each of them joined in the fun of chasing the bird again. Over and over it flew across the yard low enough so the leaping dogs could almost grab it.

Once, Bowser crashed into Handsome as they both went after the bird, their paws hitting each other's faces. At that moment, pain tore through the puppy's body. It felt like a thousand vet needles had been poked into him all at once.

For a few seconds, he lay in the corner of the yard, his brain fuzzy and dull. Then the flap of the bird's wings and the dip of her sleek body seemed enticing again and, pulling himself up, Bowser trotted back into the fray. If he threw himself into the game, he thought, he'd forget about the terrible pain. But his small body trembled with the memory.

Long before the man was aware of it the dogs sensed another human approaching. When the gray-haired woman emerged down the path across the creek, the man was still fiddling with his box so he didn't notice until she'd come up beside him. She was wearing the same bird-decorated blouse and long pants she'd had on when Bowser first saw her. Binoculars hung from her neck and she was carrying a folded newspaper.

"Mom!" he said. "What are you doing here?"

Her eyes moved over the dogs. "But there are so many here, Andrew," she said. "And they're so dirty. Isn't that blood on their feet? And there are sores on their legs."

"Don't worry. I'll fix them up before I take them back."

She batted the newspaper against her leg and looked down at the man's black box. "Well, let me see how this electric shock machine of yours works."

"Uh, I just finished with it, Mom." He was closing the lid.

"Do a little more, will you? I'm curious."

"It's not good for the dogs to overdo it." As he coiled up some wires Bowser could smell the man's nervousness with his alpha.

But, just as she'd done yesterday when the man had lied to her, she squelched the anger Bowser sensed in her. "Oh, all right then. To tell the truth, I had to steel myself to come down here anyway."

"Let me just pack up and put the dogs back in, and I'll walk back with you."

"All right, son." She took hold of one gatepost as if to test it. "Still as strong as ever. My father used to keep foxes down here, you know."

"I know."

"The cages are gone now." She looked around. "I remember Daddy packing the lumber down here on his horse. And rolls of tough wire screening. Everything he did he did well. He built this place to last."

"Yeah, it's strong."

As he arranged the black box and coiled wires in a suitcase on the ground nearby, she raised her binoculars and looked up in the trees. "Seen anything but trash birds around here?"

"No, Mom."

"I brought this down for you to look at." She lowered the binoculars and handed him the newspaper. Her eyes ranged over the dogs again and landed on Bowser. "That scruffy white one. He destroyed a snowy plover nest."

Seeing her look at him, Bowser cocked his head and pricked his small ears. She was a human female like his human. Maybe she'd love him and become his friend. But no. Not only wasn't she softening, her blue eyes seemed to grow colder as she looked at him. "I can't understand anyone letting a killer like that run wild."

"It made the front page?" the man said excitedly, as he stared at the newsprint. "This is great, Mom."

"Maybe people will open their eyes now to the damage dogs can do if they're not kept leashed." She continued to glare at Bowser, who turned around and crept away from the fence. "Look at him. He knows he did wrong."

"That mutt didn't do anything to that nest, Mom. Kharma and I set that up."

For a moment she didn't say anything, but Bowser could smell her consternation. "You?"

"Yeah."

"You killed that bird?"

"Not me myself. Kharma killed her when—"

The woman frowned. "You killed a snowy plover and destroyed its nest? Those birds are—"

"Look, Mom, a story like this is going to change people's minds. Give me a break. What I did was a great idea. Trying to retrain these mutts?" he waved toward Bowser and the others. "That's small potatoes compared to a propaganda act like this one. This is a war on behalf of birds. You can't afford to be sentimental." He entered the yard and began to shoo and drag each of the dogs back into the shed, closing the door on each one.

"Propaganda or not, I don't want any more killing of endangered birds." Her voice was loud and angry.

"All right, all right. I have some other ideas anyway." As he herded Bowser into the shed where Toro sat covering the hole, Bowser could smell the man's anxiety.

"Promise?" the woman demanded.

"I promise," he muttered.

Almost immediately after the door was locked on them, the dogs heard the outer gate being latched and the woman's irritated voice, which gradually grew fainter: "And another thing, our garbage is piling up. You promised you'd take care of it."

"Team One, resume digging," Toro commanded.

Chapter 14

Only Handsome hurried to get into position at Toro's command.

"My head still feels strange from the terrible pain, Master," Goldie whimpered, swishing her dirty tail.

"Mine too," Bowser said, as he sat down beside her. Some of the dogs sprawled on the floor of the dark shed, while others pulled leaves and seeds out of their fur or licked their sore paws. Outside the roar of the water continued, but the heat of the day had quieted the sparrows and finches. "I think bumping into each other causes that pain," Bowser said.

"It's not that," Toro said. "It's his machine."

The dogs whined their doubts.

"Yes, it is," Toro barked. "The best I can figure it, he wants us to jump up and play with his bird. When we don't, he makes us feel the terrible pain."

Bowser considered this. In the old days, before his imprisonment, his own human had sometimes made go-forth signals and urged, "Go play with Scout (or Sparky or Max)," when a strange dog visited. Maybe the man had the same urge to find playmates for his bird.

"The bird does seem to enjoy playing with us," Handsome put in, stretching each hind leg before lying down near the hole. "Did you see the gleam in her eyes?"

Goldie sighed. "That's all well and good, but are we to spend the rest of our lives being playmates for a bird?"

"No." Toro raised his hackles, showed his teeth, and growl-barked that his patience was at an end. "We are to get back to work on our hole. Team One, resume digging."

Bowser looked without enthusiasm at the shallow depression in the floor. Now he was fed and watered, he could not imagine attacking that cement-like wood with his poor splintered paws. To emphasize his youth and delicacy, he padded into a far corner, curled himself into a little ball and tried to hide behind a larger dog.

"Bowser," came Toro's bark.

Bowser raised his head feebly. "I'm too ill, Master."

"Enough of that," Toro growled. "Just now you were leaping up in the air after that bird. Now get to work."

"Yes, Master." Bowser staggered to his feet and dragged himself, weaving unsteadily through the other dogs, toward the hole. What a dumb idea of his this had turned out to be: digging through iron-hard wood and then tunneling out through dirt, which would probably be iron-hard too.

Handsome had just placed his black nose over the hole and sniffed. "It's not dirt under here. At least not right away. More like air. Outside air."

Toro came over and sniffed. "I thought this shed was flat on the dirt. But the ground underneath must slope."

Bowser scratched at a flea on his ear with vigor. Maybe there'd be room, once they were through the floor, to escape directly from under the shed. There'd be no need for more of this tedious digging. Inspired, he stretched both front paws into the hole, extended his small claws and pulled. "Yeeow!" he yelped at the pain.

"Be a dog," Toro reproached him. "Would a member of the Wild Bunch scream like that?"

"Yes, Master, if his paws hurt as much as mine," Bowser retorted, as he tentatively scratched again. "A Wild Buncher would scream even louder."

"I know the real story of the Wild Bunch," Goldie said, as she started digging. "Do you want to hear it?"

The dogs barked *yes*, although Bowser wasn't sure. There was something in Goldie's voice that made him wary.

"There were three hound brothers who lived in a town over the ridge," Goldie began. "Their human beat them regularly, and they came to hate him. One day they'd had enough. They chewed through the ropes he tied them with and ran away into the woods near Shoretown. That evening the hounds sneaked onto a ranch and killed a sheep. As they were eating it, the human who owned the sheep came out and started shooting. Two of the hounds were killed.

"The third hound escaped and came to bum around Porcupine City, where he finally got adopted by a fisherman. That dog had a good imagination and, wanting to immortalize himself and his brothers, he made up the name *The Wild Bunch* as well as all the stories that we've heard.

"Those three hounds didn't live in the woods for years, bringing down only the sick and the weak. They were caught the very first day taking down a healthy lamb who was kept in a pen. They didn't drink cold mountain water over silvery gray rocks. They didn't have coyotes as friends or run in a pack down the roads at night or any of it. They were just three young hounds from over the hill who killed a sheep and got shot at. That third dog made it all up."

Handsome looked at Goldie with dismay and whimpered, "Where did you hear that?"

"From someone who knew the third hound."

As Goldie spoke, Bowser had gradually stopped working. "But that story can't be true, Goldie. Why, the Wild Bunch—"

"Don't listen to her," Toro barked. "I know for a fact the Wild Bunch still roams the woods at night." Toro's deep howl of a voice sounded certain. "I don't doubt that we'll run into them when we escape.

"So keep digging," he added.

Goldie sighed. "I just—"

"And you, Goldie, keep your stories to yourself," Toro growled. "They're bad for morale."

"The dogs of the Wild Bunch can run faster than the fastest wolves, Master," Bowser whined. "That means they could never have been caught by humans, doesn't it."

"No, they couldn't. You're exactly right," Toro agreed. "Now, if we'll all just get back to work . . . "

The dogs continued to dig in uneasy silence. Bowser wondered why Goldie, who barked out things so frankly, would make up such a story. It must have been someone else who made it up and told her. That must be it. Of course the Wild Bunch really existed. If not—Bowser couldn't stand the empty feeling that came over him. No dog could.

"What's the first thing we're going to do when we escape?" he yipped to the others.

"I'm jumping in that creek out there," Goldie barked immediately.

"I'm going to run as fast as I can through the woods," Handsome offered.

"And I'll—" The puppy's ears flattened in dismay, and he reached to lick Handsome's mouth. "But if Goldie jumps in the creek and you run through the woods, Handsome, then we won't be together." This was almost as bad as the Wild Bunch not existing, to think of not being with the others.

"Don't worry, Bowser, we won't split up," Toro reassured him.

"Of course not, Bowser." Goldie touched his side with her paw.

"Good old Bowser," Handsome barked, and Bowser wagged his stub tail and resumed his painful job.

Chapter 15

Jenny trotted with Piccolo back to the grocery store and up the steps to the porch. "Now you stay here and keep watch," she barked gruffly. "Remember, no biting."

"No, Jenny," he barked as she retreated to sit at the foot of the steps. "You can count on me. You don't have to stay there and keep watch. I'll do it."

Almost immediately his male human came out through the screen door and attached a chain to his collar. The other end was hooked to a metal ring in the wall. After that, Piccolo could move only a short distance in any direction.

Jenny moved off, her ears forward, her tail sticking up and bristled.

"I can still do it, Jenny," Piccolo whimpered after her.

The yellow dogs Bucky and Ruby limped slowly up to sit near him on the porch. At first Piccolo glared at them, but, seeing the kind looks in their rheumy eyes, he barked, "Howdy.

"If the van comes, I want one of you to pee on it," Piccolo barked. Bucky and Ruby gave him puzzled looks. "On the tires," Piccolo said, "to lay a trail. I can't do it, tied up here."

"What van?" Ruby asked.

"The one that stole Handsome and Bowser," Piccolo said.

"I didn't know they were missing."

"Well, they are." Piccolo rolled his eyes at the ignorance of downtown dogs.

Flies and butterflies passed by occasionally. In a tall evergreen across the street some crows stood on a branch cawing. Bucky had an itchy place on his butt that he kept struggling to reach with his teeth. Eventually Ruby asked, "Why did you try to bite that man earlier?"

"I thought he was the bad man in the van."

"But he wasn't?"

"No."

Before long, Koko came trotting up. Her eyes were red. After she'd greeted Bucky and Ruby she turned to Piccolo. "Jenny told me you'd got yourself tied up and couldn't do anything if the van came by." She sat down nearby. "I'll keep watch. If you're sleepy, you may as well take a nap."

"I'm not sleepy."

"I wish I could say the same." Koko widened her amber eyes and cocked her ears in different directions. But shortly her eyelids drooped. She stood up and stretched each leg, then lay down again.

Piccolo tucked his tail between his legs. So much for making a big impression on Koko. "What did you do this morning, Koko?"

"I had to work," Koko said. "This afternoon I was going to check out Porcupine City, but I'll do that tonight if the van hasn't shown up yet."

So his mistake had ruined Koko's plans. Not only couldn't she risk taking a nap now, she was going to have to stay up most of the night again. Piccolo lay flat and looked away from her. "I'm awfully sorry, Koko," he whimpered.

He felt Koko approach and lay a paw on his shoulder. "That's okay. I expect you've learned your lesson."

The afternoon passed, Koko lightly dozing at his side and waking every time a car drove by.

Eventually his humans took his water bowl in, locked the store and unchained him. With a quick goodbye to Koko and the old yellow dogs, he trotted along between his humans, hopped in the back seat of the car, and sat quietly on the ride home. He tried to be a model dog.

"I think Piccolo's learned his lesson," his human female said that night as she and her husband sat together on the couch watching a show about humans shooting other humans. Piccolo sat on the couch between them facing the TV screen. His ears flicked at the sound of his name.

"That guy could sue the hell out of us."

"He said the skin wasn't even broken," his human female said.

Her husband rubbed his forehead and temples tiredly. "Sometimes I think the dogs in this town are more important to you females than us men."

"Don't be silly," she said and patted his knee. He put his hand over hers.

Piccolo wagged his tail slowly. He liked it when his humans touched each other.

The TV show continued, with more people being gunned down. Into Piccolo's mind came a picture of Koko out searching the dark streets of Porcupine City. Maybe they'd try to leash her. She would have to be careful. If only he could have gone with her, he could have helped watch for trouble.

The terrier stood up suddenly, preparing to jump off the couch. He would go rescue her right away. But feeling a hand on his back, he remembered. In the large scheme of things, his task was not to rescue Koko, who could probably take care of herself. His job was to be a model dog so he would not have to be tied up tomorrow.

Piccolo turned in a few circles, something his humans seemed to love, and settled back in his spot on the couch, facing the TV screen.

Although she'd not had much time to sleep after her late night excursion, Koko woke early. She made her way into the kitchen to look at her food dish. Same old kibble. She took several pieces in her mouth and carried them back to one of the living room rugs where she dropped them to eat one by one.

She'd spent most of the night scouting out Porcupine City. It was a town down the coast much like Shoretown, with small wooden houses, many of them dilapidated. She'd had a conversation with a sad husky there through the wire mesh of a shiny new fence.

"I'm trying to find two dogs who were stolen from Shoretown," Koko had low-barked. "Are you missing any dogs here?"

The gray and white husky glanced at some deep holes at the edge of the metal fence. He had obviously started to dig and given up. He didn't answer, but whined, "This new leash law is killing me. We huskies can't stand being locked up."

"What's a *leash law*?" Koko felt uneasy about the word *leash* already. Maybe *leash law* was worse.

"It means none of us get to run free any more. Our humans won't let us."

Koko's back fur bristled. "But don't they love you?"

The husky's blue eyes as he looked at her were bitter. "Yes, but they won't let us run."

"That's terrible," Koko whimpered sympathetically. So Jenny was right, she thought, even good humans could leash their dogs forever.

The husky pawed fiercely at the base of the fence, then gave up. "I've been trying for days to get out of here, but it's no use. The fence goes down too deep."

Koko remembered her mission. "Would you happen to know if any dogs are missing from Porcupine City?" she asked again.

The husky looked down the street. "A dog passing by with her human said that our alpha Toro has been gone quite a while," he low-barked. "And a golden retriever named Goldie disappeared too."

"Were they locked in their yards when they were stolen?"

"No. Their humans took them to the beach and let them run free."

"So you still get to run free sometimes?" Koko asked.

The husky's blue eyes clouded. "Not any more. Once Toro and Goldie disappeared, the humans stopped letting us out at all."

Just then a man with a flashlight had come out of the husky's house, calling, "There's a strange dog on the loose," and Koko had had to escape Porcupine City and make her way back along the empty highway to Shoretown.

The morning newspaper thunked on the front step as the Aussie picked up another pellet of boring kibble. This afternoon, after work, if she wasn't needed at the grocery store, she'd start exploring the inland towns. For now, she needed sleep.

"Kokomo." Ranger Bill emerged from the bedroom in pajamas, rubbing his ruddy face with both hands. Koko got up and followed him into the kitchen, where he measured coffee and water into a machine and pressed a button.

"I got up in the middle of the night," he said, "and you weren't around." His oddly long human feet padded down the hall. With Koko following, he opened the front door and walked down the path a few steps to pick up the newspaper. "You shouldn't run off at night, Kokomo." He stood up and looked around. The dew was still on the pink flowers of the magnolia bush and the bunch grass shone. "Oh, what a beautiful morning," he suddenly shouted in a tuneful voice. Koko yelped and jumped in excitement.

"Shall we get Michelle up to go for a walk with us before breakfast?" Ranger Bill asked.

A *walk*! Koko jumped higher, twirling in anticipation. A walk in the early morning: her favorite thing to do with humans. Ranger Bill laughed and disappeared back into the house.

Koko stood in the garden staring at the closed door. Why hadn't her humans come out yet? She ran to various windows and jumped high enough to look in. No sign of anyone, although the bedroom door was open. They must be just coming.

She ran down the path toward the road, then turned to stare at the door again. Why did it take Michelle so long to get ready? Why did she have to wear all those clothes and comb her hair and rub water and soap on her face? It took forever for a human to get from bed into the outside world.

After a few more times of running back and forth, Koko gave up and slumped down on the doorstep. She should sleep anyway. Ranger Bill must have been wrong about the walk. It couldn't possibly take Michelle this long to get ready.

But just then the door opened, and there they were.

Koko in the lead, they headed down Elm to Pine Street, passed Bushy Corner and kept going toward the big house where Michelle and Koko's patient, Mrs. Gates, lived. As they approached the mansion with its vast green lawn, gracious flowerbeds and tall spruces, Koko smelled garbage. A hard plastic garbage can lay on its side near the brick driveway. Strewn over the grass was a soggy assortment of vegetable peels, meat and fish bones, torn packaging, and other trash.

"What a mess." Michelle sighed.

"I told you so," Ranger Bill said, surveying the lawn. "Dogs just can't control themselves around garbage. I've seen this time and again."

"It could have been raccoons. Raccoons love garbage," Michelle argued. "Why do you always think it has to be dogs?"

"Because—" Ranger Bill said, as Koko lay on the grass gnawing a pork chop bone, "of this." He pounced on a small metal thing near an old banana peel, picked it up and showed it to Michelle.

Michelle looked at the metal disk, turned it over. "This doesn't make sense. Handsome's tag?"

At the sound of Handsome's name, Koko dropped the pork chop bone and stood up, flicking her ears. Why were they talking about Handsome? Had he been found? Was he home? She prowled around, sniffing harder, and another odor distinguished itself from the pungent smells of garbage—the bad man who'd taken Handsome and Bowser had been here. Yes. Her nose quivered. She could smell him clearly now. Excited, she sniffed the grass at the side of the road. Yes, the van had parked just here, where the grass was flattened. She looked hopefully up at Michelle and Bill, looked back at the flattened grass, looked at her humans again.

"Yes, Koko, some of your friends have been here," Michelle said wearily.

"This is too much," she said to Bill. "Why can't these dogs behave themselves? Here that leash law vote is coming up tomorrow night, and what do the dogs do? Handsome's gone wild, Bowser's killing snowy plovers, Piccolo's attacking strangers in town, Koko's racing off who knows where and now this." She looked at Koko angrily. "You dogs are cooking your own goose."

Michelle was mad at her for some reason. Koko lowered her body and flattened her ears in deference. How was it possible to communicate what she knew?

Then her nose gave her the answer. There were fish bones in this garbage. This garbage wasn't Mrs. Gates' garbage. It was the bad man's. He hadn't known that Mrs. Gates hated the smell of fish and wouldn't have it in her house. But Koko and Michelle knew.

Koko leapt up and darted through the strewn garbage to pick up a spiny fish bone in her mouth. She turned to show it to Michelle.

"Off, Koko, off. Drop it!" Michelle cried. "Bill, that's a fish bone. It could kill her."

As Michelle picked her way hurriedly through the garbage after her, Koko backed out of reach, the bone in her mouth, her determined eyes on Michelle.

"She's not chewing it," Michelle said. "She's just holding it. That's a relief."

When her human suddenly stopped moving toward her, Koko stopped too. Michelle said, "That's funny. I thought Mrs. Gates never ate fish. And what's this?" She picked up a damp envelope by the corner. "Look at this, Bill, it's addressed to the Nightingale Bird Sanctuary. Why would this envelope be in Mrs. Gates' garbage?"

"Who knows?" Ranger Bill said. "Mis-delivered?"

Koko dropped the fish bone and watched them. She sensed they were on to something.

"Look, Koko's dropped that fish bone. It's almost as if she were trying to tell us about this," Michelle said. "I wonder if she smells something we're not aware of."

"Sure she does. Dogs can smell a thousand times better than we can. But come on, honey, let's get on with our walk."

"Shouldn't we clean this up?" Michelle asked.

"Mrs. Gates can afford to hire some teenage kid to do that."

Koko watched as Michelle looked again at the soggy envelope. Maybe it belonged to the bad man.

But Michelle dropped it back amongst the garbage and put her arm through Ranger Bill's. As they sauntered on, Koko ran to sniff the envelope. No, it did not smell of the bad man but of some unknown female human.

Koko sighed, and turned to slowly follow her humans as they continued, still talking, occasionally raising their voices, on their walk.

Chapter 16

Thursday morning the terrier Piccolo continued his role of model dog. He ate his food immediately but with restraint, took a long thirsty drink of water and was waiting at the car when it came time for his humans to drive down to the grocery store. At the store he positioned himself on the deck just out of reach of the chain. As customers came by for the morning newspaper he wagged his tail and play-bowed, but stopped himself from jumping up or barking a greeting. He accepted the pats of women and crouched submissively for men. From inside the store came the sound of his name several times.

There was no attempt to chain him up. His good behavior had lulled his humans into forgetfulness. When no one was looking, Piccolo bristled his fur and clicked his teeth in pride.

Meanwhile he kept his eye on the street and his nose at the ready. The morning passed. On a normal morning he might have trotted down to Town Beach, stopping in at certain other stores for a free handout. But today he was on duty. Every so often another dog came by. Jenny passed three times, Rosa once.

There was no other dog in sight when the van showed up. It was dusty and gray and, when Piccolo saw it, he jumped up and growl-barked, "Grrrr-ruff." Then he told himself, *No, don't jump to conclusions. You must have proof positive. Don't let on that you suspect anything.* He let his gaze range wide, not stopping at the van, which had parked across the street. A tense cigarette-smelling man climbed out and came across the street and up the grocery store stairs.

Piccolo sniffed hard as the man passed and disappeared into the store. Then the terrier sniffed his own shoulder where he'd rubbed against Koko. Yes, this man was the one. Piccolo raced down from the porch to the street and ran across to sniff the van.

Again he craned around to check the faint remnants of burnt oil and shoe rubber he'd picked up from Koko's fur. The smells matched. This van was the one.

There was barely room under the back of the van for him to position himself, lift his leg and shoot all the pee he could muster onto the treads of a rear tire. When he straightened up, he banged his head on the oily underside and yelped.

He hurried back across the street to the porch and lapped water from his dish. He drank as fast as he could, then ran back and lifted his leg at a second tire. Nothing. He peered back toward the store. The man hadn't come out yet.

At each attempt to pee, Piccolo failed. A female cat sitting on the porch of the bakery nearby was watching him and yawning. He soft-growled, "Stupid cat, have some respect."

Finally, just as the man pushed open the grocery store door to come out, Piccolo's pee started flowing again. What a thrill to see it darken the dusty tire! He had completed his mission and done himself proud.

Afterwards, in case the bad man was watching, the terrier sauntered down the middle of Main Street toward Town Beach, his tail up and tongue hanging out, just as if it was a regular day, and he was just some no-account animal.

But as soon as the man had driven off and could no longer see him, Piccolo turned and raced out of town toward Koko's.

Koko's attention was drawn from the young pregnant therapy patient to the small brown and white terrier jumping up and down near the irises. As she watched Piccolo through the French windows, he pantomimed staring at an imaginary van, then lifting his leg to pee on a tire. She flattened her ears and opened her mouth wide to signal congratulations.

"That little dog from the grocery store seems to have the hots for Koko," the therapy patient commented. Koko saw that both the patient and Michelle were watching Piccolo.

"Shall I let Koko out?" Michelle asked.

"Oh, do," the pregnant patient said.

Wonderful of wonderfuls, Michelle suddenly stood up and opened the door.

At Piccolo's news, Koko barked high and excitedly. "Good for you, Piccolo. It's the first break in the case."

Piccolo wagged his tail hard, jumped in the air and yipped.

"Now you get back to your porch," Koko told him, "in case your humans get mad at you for running off. We don't want you tied up again. I'll let Jenny know what a cunning detective you are."

The two dogs trotted off together, splitting up at the intersection of Pine Street and Main.

Koko found the chunky alpha gnawing a bone in her overgrown yard. "Jenny, let's you and I follow Piccolo's pee trail on the van tires right after lunch."

"Take Rosa instead of me," Jenny said. "She can run faster."

"But—" Of all the dogs in Shoretown Rosa was Koko's least favorite. The spaniel always made Koko's paws sweat. "Rosa's so mean."

"Not all the time." Jenny stood up, stiffened her legs and curved her tail over her back as she leaned over Koko in a dominant stance. "This is no time for fights. Let's get over there and see if she can go."

Rosa was lying under a bush near her house. Her owners were on vacation, and she was at loose ends. "But I'd rather follow Piccolo's trail alone," she barked.

"You're tracking with Koko."

At this Rosa's lip curled slightly, but when Jenny's back fur bristled, the spaniel looked away respectfully. "All right, but she's not the boss of me."

Once they'd set out toward the highway on Piccolo's trail, Koko told Rosa, "I want us to stay off the highway as much as possible. We don't want to get rescued by humans."

"Naturally," Rosa barked. "Anyone knows that."

"Whenever possible we should travel on opposite sides of the road so if the trail turns off one of us will detect it and can bark to the other."

Rosa said, "Agreed."

"We should stay even with each other."

"Agreed."

Koko continued, feeling encouraged, "We may have to travel a long time, so to conserve energy we should travel at a moderate pace rather than full-speed."

"No," Rosa growled and came to a stop.

Koko stopped too and growled back. "Why not?"

In a nearby field a horse was pawing at ditch water, splashing it up around him, but the dogs ignored him as they stood stiff-legged, confronting each other.

Rosa barked, "The faster we run, the faster we'll get there. I can run for a long time without tiring, can't you?" The spaniel leaned challengingly toward Koko.

"Yes, but—"

"What's the fun of going if we can't run full out? I don't want to go if I can't run full out."

Koko protested, "But Jenny assigned you to—"

Rosa lifted a paw. "But I could tell Jenny, 'My paw hurts, Jenny. I can't possibly go. I'm so sorry.'" She whimpered these last words.

The fur on Koko's shoulders bristled. Of all the dogs in town, why did she have to be stuck with this one?

"All right, we can run fast," she conceded. Rosa would soon tire, she thought, being only a spaniel, and then Koko herself, with her greater Aussie endurance, could continue tracking the van herself.

No, this is wrong, Koko thought, as she sprang over a fallen tree, dashed under a hanging vine and crashed through a dense stand of coyote bush. Occasionally she glimpsed Rosa's long brown and white ears rising into the air across the road. Rosa was galloping through a sea of grasses while Koko navigated the woods. For long moments they had not bothered to check whether they were still following Piccolo's scent. The thrill of competition was too much to fight. Their lost friends, Handsome and Bowser, were forgotten.

Koko smelled fresh water, heard it rushing, dashed on and suddenly stopped short above a swift river she hadn't known existed. To the left, on the far side of a two-lane bridge, Rosa was already swimming toward the opposite shore, her dark brown head moving determinedly across the water.

Koko hesitated. She did not like water, but if she took the time to navigate the bridge, Rosa might surge ahead. Koko scrambled down the bank to the river, closed her mouth, flattened her ears, and plunged in. She paddled fast, holding her head above the rushing water. She headed for what seemed to be an island of logs and branches in the middle of the river.

First one paw, then another, touched things beneath her in the water. She tried to paddle more shallowly. In front of her face, a twisted root appeared, then vanished. When her hind foot caught on something, she yelped in surprise and yanked it free. Her panting quickened. Ahead the log island beckoned. Her heart pounding now, she paddled wildly, her paws hitting the roots and branches that were now thick in the water under and around her.

Suddenly, Koko found herself caught, her head barely above water, her body shifted to the vertical. Her front paws grabbed again and again at a tangle of slippery roots that rose to tempt her and then, when she tried to pull herself up, sank under her weight. Her hind legs flailed in the water. She thrust her head under water, trying to see what had grabbed her, and came up spluttering and whimpering, still caught.

She scream-yelped in terror. What had she done!

Chapter 17

"Koko," came Rosa's bark, "don't move."

The spaniel's dark brown head, water rippling behind, appeared on the other side of the log island. She circled wide around it and disappeared behind Koko.

Shortly Koko heard Rosa bark, "Is one of your legs caught?"

"Everything's caught."

"After I get you out of this, follow me, okay? And after this, stay away from log jams. Log jams are for birds, not dogs."

"Yes, Rosa."

As Rosa worked behind and around her, Koko felt her body pushed this way and that. Finally the tangle of waterlogged vines and branches gave way. She was once more in swimming position. She turned and paddled hard toward land.

"Careful," Rosa yelped. "You'll get caught again. I'll lead you out." The spaniel maneuvered her body around so her short brown and white tail was in front of Koko's face. "Now follow me exactly. And swim shallow."

Slowly the dogs swam through the debris. When the water around them was clear again, Rosa stopped paddling, and a current swung them slowly around in an eddy. Koko paddled harder and whimpered in alarm.

"No, Koko. Rest a minute," Rosa barked. Around and around they turned, drifting downstream. The shadow of the bridge moved over them.

Shortly Rosa signaled the Aussie, then moved out of the current and toward the far shore. Koko felt herself drawn along in the wake of the spaniel's powerful strokes.

Soon tree branches hung over them, Rosa's drenched body emerged from the water, and she clambered out of the river and up the bank. Koko stretched her paws down to feel the solid floor of the river and hurried up to dry land after the spaniel. Their stomach fur dripped as they stood gathering their strength. Then each dog shook herself, sending drops of water flying.

"You saved my life," Koko low-barked as she sank down tiredly.

"That's the first time . . . " Rosa panted, stretching on her side, "that I've felt like a real spaniel."

As swallows swooped over the river and the stones at the water's edge clicked against each other, the dogs' breathing gradually slowed. Each of them stood and shook a second time, then sat to lick themselves.

"You're certainly no water dog," Rosa barked.

"No."

"Why didn't you take the bridge?"

Koko hesitated. "I thought you'd get ahead of me."

Rosa pant-laughed. "I thought you city dogs were supposed to be so smart. Couldn't you see I *should* have gotten ahead of you? I had the easy side of the road, all grasses and weeds—it was a straight shot. You were having to run an obstacle course through the trees." She turned in a comma shape to examine her tail. "I was giving it my all. How you kept up with me I'll never know," she grumbled.

Koko looked at her companion with wonder. How could a dog be so good and so bad at the same time? "You must be terribly strong to run all out like that, then swim almost across the river, then swim back, rescue me, and across again."

Rosa tossed her long silky ears so that drops of water flew from them. "I'm a natural swimmer. My ancestors retrieved ducks who were shot by humans and fell down from the sky into the water."

"Mine herded sheep for humans. They worked all day rounding up sheep and moving them back and forth. They got to snap at bad sheep, and even bite them."

"Rescuing you is the only useful thing I've done in my life," Rosa said. "I can't even call myself a spaniel. I'm just a pet," she said with disgust.

"All a pet has to do is cock her head at her human," Koko said. Although this felt disloyal to Michelle, there was something in Rosa that brought out these half-thoughts.

"My humans went away on vacation without me," Rosa said. "Today the neighbor forgot to feed me."

"You should leave mawna on their rug." Koko herself would never have done such a thing, but she liked to imagine Rosa doing it.

Rosa high-barked, "I already chewed up one of the couch cushions."

Koko wriggled in pleasure at this wickedness. "Do they have any statues you could knock over and break?" On a small table Michelle kept a statue of a horse she constantly warned Koko not to go near. As if Koko, who had the agility bred into her to dance around the heels of a moving ram, was going to be clumsy enough to bump into a table.

"No, but I could dig up their—"

Koko yelped in alarm. In the aftermath of her near drowning and rescue, she had forgotten they must stay hidden. Michelle's car was just now crossing the bridge. It pulled to the side of the road with a squeal of brakes, and Michelle stumbled out and ran toward them. "Koko, honey. Oh, Koko, Koko. Here I am."

The dogs exchanged stricken looks. "Tonight," Koko low-barked.

"Tonight," Rosa agreed. "Pick me up as soon as you can."

The two dogs ran toward the tearful woman, wagging their stub tails, barking hello and leaping up to greet her.

And Koko could sense that even cranky Rosa delighted in that mysterious attraction that loving humans held for dogs.

For a whole day the prisoners had done nothing but sleep and work on widening the hole in the floor. As the heat of Thursday afternoon settled in, they gathered around to admire what they'd done. Through a hole as round as a large water dish they could see dusty dirt a little below floor level. The dirt was bright—light was coming from somewhere under the shed.

"You there," Toro told one of the hounds. "You've got a long neck. Try to see what's down there."

As the others backed off, the hound spread his thin front legs to either side of the hole and stuck his head down into it. His long tail waved, and he started to bay.

"Well?" Toro barked.

The hound lifted his sleek brown head. "Rabbits in the woods," he bayed to the others.

"Oh, for cats' sake," Toro protested. "Let me look."

He shoved the hound out of the way, lay on his back, flailing his great dirty legs above him, and stuck his head down the hole backwards, his throat exposed.

"There's space enough for a puppy like Bowser down here," he reported in a muffled bark. "There's daylight coming in under the shed."

When he pulled his head back up, the others saw his brown eyes were alert and hopeful. He jumped to his feet. "Bowser," he commanded. "Get down there and have a look."

Bowser approached the hole and peered in. It didn't look to him like there was much room down there. Tentatively, he stuck one front paw onto the dusty earth below, then stretched his head and other paw in. He craned to look toward the light.

Not four feet away, beyond a wire screen, were ferns and blue forget-me-nots. Beyond that were trees, their leaves sparkling in the sunlight. What a sight! What smells! If he scratched some of the dirt away, he'd have room to ease the rest of his body down and try to wiggle over to the screen.

Suddenly Bowser heard a commotion going on above. "The man's coming," Toro barked. "Cover the hole."

The puppy's hind end was roughly pushed down, and his front leg bent painfully under him. Bits of dirt fell into his face. Bowser felt a dog settle on top of the hole above him. He struggled to shake his head and sneeze out the dust in his nostrils.

"Quiet, Bowser," came Toro's bark. "The man'll hear you. We're hoping he won't notice you're missing."

Bowser set his teeth to keep from sneezing again, the dirt tickling his nose. Squeezed in the narrow space between the floor and the dirt, he felt as squashed as a run-over bug.

He heard the man open the outer gate. A delicious aroma of fresh lamb drifted in, and Bowser heard the clink of a pail. The man was bringing water and food. And not just kibble this time.

From above came sounds of the door opening and dogs running around on the floor over his head, whining and barking. The man's footsteps thumped above Bowser. He was dragging something big over the floor. His sharp voice came: "Here you go. Have a blast. I'll be back tonight to pick it up."

Bowser heard the dogs above him grunting and chewing. The smell of lamb was intoxicating. Then came another clink of a pail, the slam of the door closing and the sounds of the man moving off. Saliva rose in Bowser's mouth and dripped out onto the dirt. The man had brought a huge piece of meat!

Bowser listened. From above came thunks and growls. The dogs must be gorging on the lamb. They'd completely forgotten Bowser. He could no longer feel anyone sitting above him, but when he tried to move he was stuck. His leg hurt.

"What about me?" he whined loudly.

"Just stay where you are," Toro barked from above.

Bowser could tell that the big dog's mouth was full. "Everyone else gets to gorge on lamb, and all I get is a mouthful of dirt."

He barked once, waited, barked again, waited, barked again.

There was no reply other than the sounds of dogs tearing and chewing meat.

No dog needed these jerks as friends. Using all his strength and ignoring the pain, Bowser wrenched his front leg out from under him, tested it—it didn't hurt that much—and scrabbled toward the screen and the greenery outside. He would break through the screen and head for home all by himself. Ha! It would serve the rest of them right.

He butted the top of his small head against the screen and pushed. Bits of dust and dirt fluttered down, but the screen didn't budge. He planted his front paws, extended his claws into the dirt and strained harder.

"The screen doesn't move," he whined.

When there was no response," he barked loudly, "The screen doesn't move."

"Try to dig under it." Toro's deep voice sounded close. He must have stationed himself over the hole.

Bowser scratched with one front paw at the crumbly soil. Every time a claw caught in the metal mesh of the screen, pain shot up his leg. He dug a small investigatory hole, then clawed deeper and deeper. "The screen goes way into the dirt," he barked.

"Keep digging," Toro ordered.

Bowser's claws hit something solid. He felt around with his footpad. Whatever was there was hard and cold. "It feels like rock." He widened the hole. "A shelf of rock."

"And the screen goes right to it?"

Bowser pushed away more dirt and peered into the hole. "Yes."

"Can you force your paw under the screen?"

Bowser tried. "No, it's too tight."

There was silence. "Curses," Toro burst out. Bowser heard him stalking around above. There were a few yelps, whimpers and then silence.

While he waited for whatever would happen next, Bowser lay with his chin on his paws looking out through the screen. A fly's wings shone as it meandered by. Through the leaves of the trees he saw a squirrel on a branch. To the far right he caught a glimpse of spray from a waterfall.

"Bowser?" came Handsome's low-bark.

"What?" Craning his head around, he could just make out Handsome's black nose sticking down through the hole.

"Here. We saved you some tender meat." There was a plop of something hitting the dirt. Bowser smelled lamb. "Can you reach it?"

"I'll try," Bowser wagged his stub tail. "Is Toro—?"

"Yes, he's loco again."

The two dogs conferred. "What are we going to do, Handsome?" Bowser whimpered.

"There's no hope of getting out?"

"Not here."

"You're a digging dog. What do you think?" Handsome asked.

The terrier liked being described as a *digging dog*. He considered. "This dirt is dry and easy to dig," he began. "There are beams of wood holding up the floor. I could dig under them to another part of the shed and see what's there."

"Dog-gone-it, you're smart, Bowser," Handsome low-barked. "First, eat this lamb. Up here we'll be napping. Maybe when Toro wakes up, he'll be better again."

After he'd eaten, Bowser worked quietly, digging the dirt from under one of the support beams. Soon he had a space wide enough to see through. But the view was dismaying. There was another open space just like the one he was in, and another beam beyond that. It was like looking from one prison cell into the next.

Bowser sighed. Who was he kidding? They were not going to get out this way. The failure of their plan had driven Toro loco. If Bowser were smart, he'd go loco too. He whimpered softly and sank his chin onto his paws. Maybe he'd die down here. Such a tragically short life. Never to have known real power or love or been a father to pups. To die under a shed like a common possum . . .

"But, Master, you can't—" Bowser heard Goldie bark sharply. It was just sunset and the trees glowed reddish through the screen.

"Yes, I can," came Toro's growl. "It's obvious that stupid pup's plan isn't working out. This time I'll go for the man's throat."

Go for his throat! Under the shed Bowser flattened his small ears and whimpered.

"But, Master," Goldie said, "how will we get out of the yard? The man always locks it now."

Toro growled, "That's exactly why I must kill him. That way we will have plenty of time to dig under the fence."

Kill him! Bowser's heart pounded.

"But, Master, our humans may save us," Handsome barked.

"They haven't yet, have they? And some of us have been here for awfully long."

Suddenly Bowser remembered the meeting at Bushy Corner where the Shoretown dogs had looked at Handsome's picture. "There's Jenny and Koko. They may find us," he whined.

There was a scuffling noise above, and Toro's big face appeared in the hole. "Have you found a way out, Pup?"

Bowser looked away submissively from the wild-eyed dog. "No, Master. But Jenny's our alpha, and Koko's a city dog who knows how to find us." He wondered if this was true. What was a *city dog*, anyway? "They'll come and save us."

"Yes, Master," he heard Handsome agree. "Koko will save us."

"Ridiculous," Toro growled, and resumed his stalking around the shed. "You're all like so many sheep.

Waiting, waiting, to be rescued. You're not dogs, you're chipmunks. I'm glad I'm not one of you."

"But Toro, if you kill the man you'll probably be killed too," Handsome whined.

"We'll see. Oh, I won't be such a fool as to go home to Porcupine City. I'll live in the woods far from here. And even if humans should hunt and kill me, I will have saved you all, just as I promised. I will have completed my mission."

Bowser thought hard. If the bad man was killed by a dog, how would humans know that it was Toro who'd killed him? Maybe they'd blame him, Bowser. Maybe they'd think Handsome did it. Bowser whined, imagining himself and Handsome with a shotgun pointed at their heads.

Someone must do something.

But it was hard to think what.

Chapter 18

It was that evening. Two tired thirsty dogs, one a Springer spaniel, the other an Australian shepherd, trudged up a curving dirt road through a woods rich with bird song and animal smells.

"The bad man's van must be parked at the top of a blasted mountain," Rosa growled.

"There's something up ahead." Koko peered through the gathering darkness.

Soon the faint scent that Piccolo had left on the van's tires veered off the road onto gravel, and the two dogs stood before a gate in a high wooden fence. To the left of the gate was a sign with pictures of birds.

They shoved and pulled at the gate with their teeth, but it wouldn't budge. Giving up, they turned to barge through the growth that lined the fence, banging their paws on rocks and picking up burrs and seeds in their fur. The moon was rising in the dark blue sky as the long fence finally ended, and the two dogs pushed through thick brush onto an animal path.

Both dogs raised their noses and sniffed the cooling air, which was delicious with the smells of night animals coming out from their burrows.

"There it is. The bad man's smell," Koko suddenly low-barked. "And Handsome's." Her heart leapt.

Rosa's brown nose quivered. "Bowser's around too."

The two dogs hurried in the direction of the dog scents.

After they'd run a good distance and descended a long hill, there came, out of the night, a familiar puppy yip: "I smell Koko. And Rosa. I told you Koko would come."

The two newcomers exchanged a silent signal, then padded quickly and quietly across a bridge of planks toward a strong-smelling shed. Koko sensed wary dogs inside. At the same time, the man's odor grew stronger.

"Who's out there?" challenged an unfamiliar dog.

Koko signaled to Rosa to stay quiet.

"It's Koko and Rosa, Master," came Handsome's bark. "They've come all the way from Shoretown to rescue us." His voice became loud and cheerful. "Koko, are you there?"

Koko longed to greet him, but she stayed silent as she and Rosa prowled around the fenced yard to the back of the shed. It was better the man shouldn't know they were there. A strange bark might alert him.

"Koko and Rosa, I see you," came Bowser's yip from under the shed. Moving closer to the building, Koko saw his small white face staring through a screen.

"See if there's any way for them to escape," Koko low-barked to Rosa who had already begun to examine the perimeter of the shed.

"How many of you are in there?" Koko asked Bowser.

"Lots of us. The bad man hardly ever feeds us, and we have to sleep in our own mawna," Bowser barked righteously.

Koko warned, "Bowser, that man's headed this way. We smelled him coming down the hill."

The puppy seemed to shrink. "Do something, Koko. As soon as the bad man opens the door, our alpha, Toro—" Bowser turned to look back fearfully, "—he's going to kill him."

Koko's red fur stood up. "Your alpha is loco?"

Up to now, Koko had kept her bark low, but this was an emergency. "Handsome?"

"Hello, dear Koko," came Handsome's familiar warm woof.

"The man's coming. He'll be here any minute."

"But—"

"You know what you have to do, Handsome. You've got to stop that loco dog who's planning to attack."

"Master is prepared to die to save us, Koko. He's decided we can't escape any other way."

"Of course you can," Koko barked. "Rosa and I see a great escape hole, don't we, Rosa?"

Rosa barked in agreement, although it was clear as she scratched the dirt at the base of the shed that she hadn't found much yet.

"Fate has determined that the man must die," came a roar from Toro. "There is no other way out."

"Toro," Koko barked. "I understand how you feel. It must be terrible in there. But, believe me, there is another way." She glanced toward the corner of the shed where the ground seemed to have fallen away into the creek. Rosa was stretching her neck to examine the corner of the building. Her short brown and white tail wagged. "Listen to me, Toro. There's a weakness at the corner of the shed near the creek."

"My ancestors have spoken to me. The man must die," Toro howled.

Koko's heart pounded. "Handsome?"

"Yes, Koko?"

"You and the other dogs must stop Toro. I know he's powerful and certain, but, Handsome, he's wrong!"

"But he's our alpha," came another dog's bark. "It's not right to overthrow an alpha."

"You see, Koko?" came Toro's proud howl. "My dogs are loyal to me."

"*Your* dogs," Koko barked. "Are all of you dogs inside there *Toro's* dogs?"

She heard whimpering. "No," Handsome barked, "But he's our alpha."

"Yes, he's your alpha, but isn't an alpha supposed to act like a *father*? If you and I had puppies, Handsome, would you kill a human and get shot dead, when your puppies needed you? No, you—"

She broke off as she heard the man unlocking the gate to the fenced yard. She raced around the shed and barked at him, "Don't go in. One of the dogs is going to attack. Don't do it."

But the man raised a stick he was carrying, and the Aussie had to jump aside as he swung it at her. Again she lunged at him, grabbing his muddy pant leg with her teeth. This time the man kicked out, his boot hitting her hard in the chest. Koko was flung into the dirt outside the gate, the wind knocked out of her. She lay trying to catch her breath.

"Koko, are you okay?" Rosa's long spaniel ears caressed Koko's face.

Koko wanted to tell her, "Stop the man." But the Aussie couldn't breathe, much less bark.

It was too late in any case, for the gate just then snapped shut against them.

The man made his way up to the door. He leaned his stick against the shed, twisted the padlock, moving it first one way, then the other, then back. He tugged at it, but it didn't open. Muttering, he pulled a small flashlight from his pocket and, holding it in his mouth so the beam lit up the padlock, tried again. This time the padlock swung open, and he pulled at the door handle as he reached for his stick.

What happened then was so frightening Koko and Rosa yelped in terror. A huge black and brown dog came flying from the darkness, his long white teeth pointed straight at the man's throat. In the same instant, the man screamed and raised his stick. The dog seemed to stop in midair, then crash down in a tangle of legs and dog heads.

The door slammed upon the man's back. From inside came his angry shouts and the frightened yelps and whines of dogs.

Koko and Rosa crouched together, staring in dismay. Shortly, the door cracked open, and the man backed out of the shed, dragging a sheep carcass. After locking up, he stood in the yard, leaning over with his hands on his knees, breathing hard. From inside came more whines and whimpers.

Koko watched with Rosa as the man pulled a large black plastic bag from his pocket and thrust the mutilated sheep carcass into it. Again he opened and relocked the gate and, swinging the heavy bag over his thin shoulder, slowly moved away across the plank bridge and up the path.

When she judged the man was well away, Koko barked, "What's going on in there?"

Toro upbraided her. "Now, look what you've done, Koko. I was willing to give my life for their freedom. Instead, they stopped me from attacking by practically pulling my leg off."

"Don't blame Koko," Handsome protested, and one of the other imprisoned dogs barked, "For dogs' sake, Toro, we just saved your life. Stop complaining."

Koko noticed that the dogs were no longer calling Toro *Master.*

"I was not committed enough," Toro barked. "If I'd been perfectly committed, not even a hundred dogs could have stopped me. Why, my ancestors—"

"Look," Koko interrupted, "Rosa and I have found a weakness under the corner of the shed next to the waterfall. The rock shelf is crumbling there. If you can make your way to that corner you should be able to jump out into the creek."

"Jump into the creek?" Toro yowled. "How far?"

"The height of a tall man."

"Into water?"

"I've jumped that far," Handsome barked.

As the dogs inside argued, Koko and Rosa conferred. The part of the creek into which the dogs would have to jump was currently crowded with branches. If the escapees were to avoid breaking their legs, they'd need a pool cleared.

Koko skidded down the steep bank after Rosa and gingerly stepped into the cold water. Rosa gripped the end of one of the dead limbs in her teeth, straightened her legs and yanked.

Koko grabbed the same branch with her teeth and together the two dogs maneuvered it to the edge of the creek. "We're clearing you a place to jump into," Koko barked.

The squabbles and whining inside the shed quieted. Gradually there came the sounds of dogs digging and scraping wood.

"Those dopes have finally gone to work," Rosa growled, as she headed for yet another waterlogged branch.

Shortly they heard an excited yip from Bowser, "I'm on the other side of the first beam."

Owls hooted, then hunted silently in the moonlit woods. There came a smell of a dying animal, and another of rabbits being born.

Once, from the shed, came the baying cry of the smaller hound. He had made it down through the widened hole in the floor and was digging out a space for the larger dogs.

Shortly after that, Koko and Rosa flopped down on the steep bank of the rushing creek. "Dogs," Koko called. "Rosa and I have cleared you a pool to jump into at the base of the waterfall. There are some rocks, so be careful. Now we have to get back home, before our humans miss us."

"We'll make it, Koko," Handsome cried. "There's no stopping us now."

"Come home as fast as you can," Koko barked. "We'll have a wonderful run together," she added, with a tender grunt and racing of her heart.

"Goodbye, Koko and Rosa," Bowser yipped. "See you tomorrow back in Shoretown."

"Goodbye and good luck," Koko and Rosa barked, as they trotted tiredly over the bridge of boards to begin the long run home.

Chapter 19

"I think you all should know," Toro's muffled voice came from above to the dogs digging under the floor, "that a member of the Wild Bunch just spoke to me in a vision."

Bowser stopped digging under the last beam and listened closely. How he would love a Wild Buncher to appear to him.

"He warned me to beware of a red dog who will lead us to leap into the water to our deaths."

"Koko is reddish brown," Bowser barked loudly. "He couldn't have meant Koko, could he, Toro?"

"Koko is red?" Toro exclaimed. "I didn't know that."

"Yes, you did. Handsome told us when Koko first arrived," Goldie corrected him. "You just made that vision up because you're scared to jump into the creek."

"I am not scared," Toro roared. "And a Wild Buncher did speak to me. Who are you to challenge one of my visions?"

"I guess you want us to believe that Koko's plan for us to jump into the creek is some fox trick. Well, I, for one, don't believe it. She and Rosa worked a long time clearing out those branches."

"A man's height is a long jump for a dog," Toro argued. "And there are rocks on the floor of that creek, she said so herself."

"Well, it's our only chance for escape, and so I'm jumping," Handsome barked.

"I'm jumping too," Bowser barked back, although he felt a little faint at heart. If a Wild Buncher had warned them against it . . .

"If you want to ignore my vision . . . " Toro grumbled, and Bowser heard him throw himself onto the floor.

"How are you coming, Bowser?" Goldie barked from behind him.

Bowser blinked the dirt from his eyes. The night had been punctuated with howls of celebration as the dogs struggled down through the hole in the floor and maneuvered under the beams toward the escape corner. Now, the puppy saw he'd dug a big enough space to wriggle under the last beam. He squeezed himself through and barked, "I see the escape hole."

He flattened himself against the dirt and wriggled to the gap under the screen. The rock shelf under the corner of the building had crumbled. Close by, the noisy waterfall roiled and frothed. Bowser pulled back in fright, then craned his head forward again. Far below, at the base of the waterfall, was a small patch of smooth water. That must be where Koko and Rosa had meant for him and the others to jump. *A Wild Buncher would throw himself down into that dog-dish-sized spot immediately*, Bowser told himself. But he felt faint.

He trembled there on the edge of the gap until Handsome and Goldie joined him. The two bigger dogs stood on the edge unconcernedly, looking down. They crouched to scratch at the rotten rock shelf, chipping off chunks that splashed down into the rushing water. The gap grew wider. Once Handsome slipped, and Goldie pulled him back by the scruff of the neck. "I want to go first. I love jumping into water," the golden retriever volunteered.

"I love it too. I'll go second." The Lab loosened a particularly large chunk of rock and sent it crashing below.

"Yes, Goldie and Handsome, you two go first," Toro barked from behind. "I'll guide the other dogs from back here."

The sky was just beginning to lighten when Goldie deemed the gap wide enough for her big body. Bowser felt sick to his stomach now the moment was at hand. He crept forward and opened his mouth to wish her luck. But too late—she had already plunged down and was flailing on her side, the water pushing her downstream amongst the foam and rocks.

"Goldie," Bowser yelped, from his spot near the gap. If even Goldie, who loved water, couldn't make it . . .

But shortly he saw the golden retriever stagger up and make her way back upstream in the shallows. She stood catching her breath, then waded up to her shoulders in water. "I hit my foot on a rock we must have knocked down just now." She dived, the water swirling around her. Soon a sharp rock appeared, Goldie's nose nudging it along toward the bank. "Okay," she called. "Next?"

Bowser's claws clung hard to the dirt floor as Handsome pushed through the gap, straightened out and landed in the churning water with a loud smack, his legs spread. He half-swam, half-waded downstream, taking great gulps of water "Come on in," he barked back cheerfully. "The water's fine."

Once Handsome had jumped, it was Bowser's turn. Below him the calm patch of water seemed the size of a doughnut.

"Come on, Pup," Goldie barked. "I'll be right here if you need me."

"Why don't I let someone else go first," Bowser whimpered, and then—had there been a little push from the shepherd behind him?—he was falling, falling, falling. He landed headfirst, his legs scrabbling to get a grip on the air. As he was propelled down through the water, he inhaled and choked. One front paw banged against something hard. Then he felt the scruff of his neck grabbed, and he was pulled up to cough in the fresh air. Goldie hauled him to shore where he struggled to his feet. "There you go, Pup." The golden licked his face with her big purple tongue.

Handsome was waiting for him on the creek bank in a play bow, his rump in the air, his front legs bent. Bowser scrambled up the bank, nipped Handsome's ear, and the two dogs chased each other into the woods and back, stopping now and then to stare at each other in expectation.

Goldie joined them, and the three of them darted after butterflies, sniffed at animal holes and splashed back into the creek, while the rest of the captive dogs leapt down one by one. Finally, only Toro remained looking down from the gap under the shed.

"Toro?" Goldie cajoled. "We should be on our way in case the man comes back."

There was no answer.

Bowser and Handsome stopped playing and moved upstream to stand in the foaming water with the rest of the dogs looking up at Toro's worried face. "I don't know if I should jump, what with this leg you practically tore off me."

"Your leg will be fine," Goldie barked. "Look, I'm the only one who hit a rock, and I moved it."

"Because of my superior build, I might land differently," Toro persisted.

"But, Toro, don't you want to escape?" Goldie asked. "We'll help you if anything goes wrong."

Bowser peered up at Toro. Was it possible Toro was afraid? It couldn't be. Toro was a strong fierce dog, ready to attack a man and give his life for others. Yet he looked now as frightened of jumping as Bowser had been. "Master, I'll help you," the terrier yipped, swimming to the spot where Goldie had waited for him.

At that, Toro's fearful expression slowly changed to one of resolution. "Thank you, Pup. You're right. I am Master." A moment later he came flying down through the air, landed with hardly a splash, disappeared and rose up again. He scrambled up to shore on his strong legs, and after two grand shakes, resumed his air of command. "Now that I've brought us all this far, we must get a move on. Bowser, stand tall. It may not be long before we meet the Wild Bunch and you must look your best."

"What does Toro mean about meeting the Wild Bunch?" Bowser asked Handsome as the dogs circled the fenced yard and crossed the plank bridge.

"Beats me." Handsome stopped to sniff at a bush, then an animal hole. "Isn't this super? We're headed home, Bowser. Home."

When the dogs came to the fence that surrounded the preserve, Handsome and Bowser turned to follow Koko and Rosa's trail back to Shoretown, but Toro stopped them. "That's too risky, too close to humans. We must get away from this evil place and head deeper into the woods before we turn toward home."

"But Toro," Handsome protested. "Bowser and I want to go home right now and get something to eat and see our humans."

"Of course you do. I want to return to Porcupine City too. But it would be stupid to get caught by the man again after we've been through so much. We must head deeper into the woods. Besides, there's a chance we may meet the Wild Bunch. They sometimes show themselves to other heroic dogs."

Bowser was thrilled to hear this. "Other heroic dogs"—that meant him. Sure, he longed to lick his human's face again, but couldn't he postpone that wonderful event? Wouldn't it make the reunion even more poignant? Besides, after she'd fed him some delicious food—Bowser drooled—his human would want to give him a bath.

"You two run on home to Shoretown," Goldie urged them. "Don't listen to Toro."

The puppy and the Lab looked at each other, then at Toro, then at Goldie. "You really think we might meet the Wild Bunch?" Bowser asked Toro.

Goldie snapped angrily. "You dogs and your stupid Wild Bunch. Toro may say he's eager to get back to Porcupine City, but he's not. As soon as our humans see us, they'll leash us. All the dogs in Porcupine City are leashed now. Toro's just trying to get you to stay with him. I told you, the Wild Bunch never existed. It's just a story."

"Of course they existed," Toro roared, "and still do."

At that moment the dogs' decision was made for them. As one, their noses sniffed the air: a deer had strayed nearby. They could hear the faint rustle of leaves as it browsed.

It was as if they lost thousands of years of domestication right then. The hounds took off baying and eight dogs streaked into the woods after them, their route home and all else forgotten in the thrill of the chase.

Chapter 20

Her eyes scratchy from being out so late, her mouth sore from dragging branches out of the creek, Koko padded along behind Michelle and Ranger Bill. Exciting as it normally would have been to go for yet another morning walk, she would have preferred to stay home and catch up on her sleep. The musty scent of an old raccoon who'd recently crossed the dirt road was irritating.

As far as Koko knew, Bowser and Handsome still hadn't made it back to Shoretown. What was keeping them?

"Koko, why so low-energy this morning?" Michelle asked.

Koko, hearing her name and sensing Michelle's reproach, sped up to sniff the dust-covered weeds by the road with feigned interest. She knew Michelle counted on her to display high spirits. Sure enough, as soon as Koko cocked her ears and let her tongue hang out, Michelle started humming a tune.

They passed the Gates' place—the lawn was smooth and green again, all signs of yesterday's garbage gone—and headed down toward the sheep meadow.

As a turkey buzzard swept over them, going in the same direction, Ranger Bill frowned and started walking faster.

At the same moment Koko smelled lamb. She raced ahead, dashing through the grasses beside the road, and, finding a new hole under the barbed wire fence, squeezed through into the sheep meadow. There, not ten feet away, was a gnawed-on sheep carcass with three turkey vultures pecking at it. Koko barked sharply, and they rose in a fit of beating wings and settled down again, one on a fencepost, the other two on the stubble nearby.

Koko examined the carcass. It was the same one the man had dragged out of the shed last night. Her hackles rose, and she looked around in alarm. To the humans this scene would look like dogs had killed and eaten a sheep. Dogs would be blamed. Ranger Bill was striding down the road towards the gate and Michelle was not far behind.

Koko heard the faint screech of the gate as Ranger Bill and Michelle reached the meadow. Skimming the tatters of yellowing fur and bloody meat with her nose, Koko started a thorough search of the dead animal. At the mangled neck, she found an odor of burnt flesh and metal. The odor had something to do with humans, she was sure. Propping her paws in the bloody chest cavity, Koko yanked at the flesh of the sheep's throat.

"Koko, stop that," Michelle yelled. Out of the corner of her eye Koko saw the humans break into a run toward her.

She pulled off a hunk of flesh and swallowed it whole, took another bite, and another. Now the burnt smell was stronger. Koko plunged her head into the sheep's chest.

Ranger Bill dived to grab her, but Koko, still gnawing at the sheep, sidestepped. He lunged again; she jumped away, pulling the carcass with her. The burnt smell was intense. She opened her mouth and chomped deeper into the sheep.

And felt her teeth close on something small and hard.

"Koko!" Reaching for her, the two humans staggered as she suddenly dropped the carcass, sat down, and looked up at them. The little hard thing was safe in her mouth.

"Koko," Michelle cried, catching her balance against Ranger Bill. "You're covered with blood."

Breathing hard, Ranger Bill reached down and fumbled for Koko's collar. She shifted a little to make it easier for him.

"She's such a carnivore," Michelle exclaimed.

Squatting and holding Koko at arm's length, Ranger Bill stared grimly at the carcass. "Michelle, you're not going to like this," he said, "but she's not the only dog who's been at this thing."

Michelle stared too. "Dogs did that?"

His eyes went to the fence. "Look at that," he said, moving a few steps toward it, crouching down and pulling a tuft of fur from the barbed wire. "That's not coyote fur. Looks like a golden retriever. And this bit's from a terrier."

Afraid the little thing she'd dug out of the sheep would fall out of her mouth, Koko couldn't bark. Instead she growled to get the humans' attention.

"Quiet, Koko," Michelle said. "I never knew she had such a blood lust. It's unsettling. Look at the blood on her face."

"You get a pack of dogs together, that blood lust can lead to this," Ranger Bill said. "You're not going to be able to stop that leash law from passing tonight after this." He stood up. "Speaking of which, put her on a leash, will you? I don't want her attacking this thing again."

Leash, leash—Ranger Bill was always talking about *leashes*. Michelle gave Koko a long hard look; Koko gave her a similar look back.

"I didn't bring a leash," Michelle said.

Ranger Bill sent out sparks of annoyance. "You've got to remember to bring a leash, sweetheart."

"You can let her go. She's okay now. Look, she's being as good as gold." Michelle leaned closer to Koko. "Koko, have you got something stuck in your mouth?"

Koko opened wide, and Michelle crouched down. "Did you get a bone caught in there? Hold still now." Michelle did her usual pill-giving trick of pressing Koko's cheek skin against her teeth with one hand while reaching into her mouth with the other. "Icck, your fur's so sticky, honey." Koko felt Michelle's fingers move around, then fasten on the small hard thing.

Michelle stood up, peered at it. "Bill, it's a bullet."

He took it from her and stared at it, frowning. "Where'd she get that?"

"I don't know." Michelle looked at Koko. "From inside that sheep?"

Koko stared into Michelle's eyes. She saw how important the small hard thing was to the humans. Hopefully they'd connect it to the bad man. Metal was always useful to humans, every dog knew that.

Bill prodded the carcass with his boot. "Too chewed-up to see if it was shot." He reached down to grab hold of a stiff leg and fling the body over. "Who's crazy enough to shoot a sheep and then not make away with it anyway? No, Koko must have had that bullet stuck in her teeth. Probably picked it up during one of her adventures. Right, Koko?" He smiled at her, and Koko gave him a bright look in return.

"Maybe, but it seems to me something fishy's going on."

Koko caught the word *fish,* and felt discouraged. What did *fish* have to do with anything?

Now the humans were moving back toward the gate. Koko gave a last angry bark at the vultures and trotted after them, trying to lick her bloody cheeks as she walked. It was impossible to walk and clean herself at the same time, and she ended up sitting and repeatedly licking the side of her paw to rub against her cheek. Of course the humans didn't wait for her, just called her name irritably again and again.

A few minutes later, while Ranger Bill went in to talk to Russ Harding, the man who owned the sheep, Michelle stood toeing the gravel in the Hardings' driveway. At one point she knelt down, held Koko's face in her hands and looked into her eyes. "Are you trying to tell us something, Koko?" Although she didn't understand the words, Koko thought that at that moment everything she knew might be passing directly into Michelle. She continued to give Michelle her most intense stare until Ranger Bill returned.

On the walk home, Koko heard the humans use the word *bird* several times. She danced around their legs excitedly, remembering the picture of birds near the bad man's gate. Maybe Michelle suspected him.

But just as she started to feel hopeful, the voices of the two humans grew louder.

Koko sighed. Humans angry at each other were no use at all—it was like Jenny said, this was no time for fights. As they passed the dirt road where Bowser lived, the Aussie took a small running detour to check if he'd arrived home yet. But there was no sign or smell of him.

"That dog of yours is completely out of control," Ranger Bill said, as Koko trotted back to join them.

"She is not!"

"Is too!"

"Is not!"

Koko ran ahead of her two humans, looked up, licked her lips, yawned, looked aside—gave them all the calming messages she knew—but for the rest of the walk they didn't speak to each other. A few minutes after they got home Ranger Bill climbed into his truck and slammed the door, causing both Koko and Michelle to flinch.

"Don't worry, he's just upset." Michelle said, as they got ready for work, Michelle changing her clothes and Koko cleaning the last bits of sheep blood from her cheeks and paws. "He'll be back at noon, you'll see."

Chapter 21

By late that morning, Koko was finding it hard to keep her attention on Michelle's therapy clients. At the slightest stirring in the garden, the Aussie half-stood, hoping to catch sight of Bowser and Handsome. Where were they? Had they not been able to get out of the shed after all? Had one of them broken a leg jumping into the creek? Had the man caught them again? Were they lost? Koko brooded over these scenarios, her eyes fixed unseeingly on the lonely-smelling woman on the couch.

There was movement among the irises, and Koko jumped to her feet.

But it was only Jenny, signaling that Handsome and Bowser had not returned. The sun was almost overhead. Where were they?

"Down, Koko," Michelle said. "I'm sorry," she continued to the woman on the couch. "Koko's been so jumpy today. It's as if she knows that leash law vote is coming up tonight."

"Yes, I'm going to vote for that," the woman said. "It's so hard on people when their dogs run off."

Koko sensed Michelle stiffen, but her voice continued clear and encouraging.

When Ranger Bill's truck turned into the drive at lunch time, Koko ran to greet him. He tousled her head and called her Kokomo, as if he'd forgotten all about being mad.

Michelle ran out of the house with a paper bag, urged Koko up into her cramped place behind the truck seats, and jumped in after her. Ranger Bill took off, scattering gravel. From the paper bag Michelle took delicious-smelling sandwiches for her and Ranger Bill, and, for Koko, two stale milkbones.

The truck sped along. Koko, licking the crumbs off her cheeks, saw out the window that they were on the same road she and Rosa had traveled the night before. To avoid feeling woozy as the scenery flashed by, she focused her eyes on a distant cloud.

When the truck missed the turn up the hill to the shed, Koko yelped loudly in protest.

"Quiet, Koko." Michelle turned to glare at her. "I'm sorry, Bill."

Koko barked as loud as she could in Ranger Bill's ear. "Turn around," she barked. "You fool," she barked. Despite the reverence she usually had for humans this kind of stupidity was intolerable. "You dope," she barked. "This is the place."

"Shut up, Koko," Michelle yelled.

"But that was the road," Koko barked. "Handsome, Bowser—they might still be there, up that road."

Then Michelle did a mean thing. She reached back to grab Koko's nose and hold her jaws closed so all she could do was whimper.

As Koko banged from side to side in her spot behind the seats, she eyed the vulnerable backs of the humans' necks. If their roles had been reversed, and she, Koko, had owned a truck and been able to drive, would she have clamped her paw over Michelle's mouth when Michelle had something terribly important to say? Would she have forced Michelle to sit in this cramped uncomfortable place, knocking herself every time the truck went around a curve? Would she have given Michelle stale milkbones while she herself ate a turkey sandwich? Good as Michelle was for a human, she still treated Koko like a farm animal.

Koko stood stiffly angry. Eventually, when the swaying of the truck and her own tiredness caused her eyelids to grow heavy, she sank to the floor behind the seats.

After that, she was only half-aware of the stops and starts as the truck encountered more traffic.

When Ranger Bill pulled to the curb, Koko struggled to stand up. She saw Michelle get out of the truck and cross the sidewalk to climb the steps of a large white building.

They drove on without Michelle, Koko looking back anxiously, and shortly pulled up in a neighborhood with green lawns and sunny driveways. The Aussie jumped into the front seat, ready to leap out, but Ranger Bill just patted her head, cracked the two side windows and locked her in again.

There was nothing to do but lie and wait.

The air grew hotter as Koko slept. She woke, panting, to the sound of Ranger Bill unlocking the truck.

"Where's Michelle?" Koko whimpered, as the truck moved off again.

And then she saw her beloved human, yellow jacket slung over a shoulder, smiling and sticking her thumb out as she waited by the curb. After Michelle had jumped in, Koko put her paws up on the back of the seat and leaned to lick her cheek in greeting.

As the truck moved out into traffic, Ranger Bill said, "The sheriff thought the bullet was from an old shotgun fired recently. He's sending it in for tests."

Koko knew the rhythm of human conversation and turned her attention to Michelle.

"Old Mr. Nightingale used to run a fox farm. I wonder if he had a shotgun."

There was that word *Nightingale* again.

"Could be. A lot of folks kept shotguns in his day. Of course, Old Man Nightingale *kept* foxes, he didn't *shoot* them."

"I know, smarty-pants." Michelle leaned over and kissed him on his prickly cheek. Then, settling back, she said, "I stopped at both County Records and the library. The

116

Nightingale estate is 4000 acres of prime land, owned free and clear for over a hundred years. Developers have offered enormous sums, but Mrs. Nightingale is never interested. She was educated at Swarthmore in Pennsylvania, married a test pilot who died on the job, had one son, Andrew, and has never remarried. She's enormously wealthy, devoted to saving birds and has always given generously to environmental causes."

"Nothing really new there."

"No. But listen to this. I fell into conversation with a young librarian who used to know Andrew, Mrs. Nightingale's son. She'd seen him recently, she said. He was showing off his trained bird in a local park. And, get this, one of the things she saw the bird do was tempt a dog into chasing it. It was quite amazing, she said. The bird swooped down in front of a dog and the dog couldn't resist running after it. She was quite impressed."

"Strange thing to train a bird to do," Ranger Bill said as he turned onto the highway back toward Shoretown.

"I thought so too. Do you suppose Andrew Nightingale's using that bird to trap our dogs? What do you say we stop at the bird sanctuary on our way home?"

During this exchange, Koko had heard the words *bird, dog* and *Nightingale* with rising excitement. Along with a strong hunting instinct that she sniffed in the humans, their words seemed hopeful. *Nightingale* might mean "bad human."

When Ranger Bill, on the way back to Shoretown, turned onto the bad man's road, Koko struggled to jump into the front seat and lick his and Michelle's faces in thanks.

But almost immediately her paws started to sweat, and she sat back down, for through the cracked windows of the truck came the strong scents of three dogs who were supposed to be in Shoretown. What were Jenny, Rosa and Piccolo doing here? Had they been captured too and brought up this road in the van? Were all the dogs from Shoretown prisoners now?

When they reached the closed gate, Michelle and Ranger Bill left the truck and stood fiddling with a box on the wooden fence. The minutes passed. Koko barked once, and Michelle turned to look at her. Koko stared at the brush that she and Rosa had burrowed through along the fence.

Michelle turned and looked the same way. "I'm going to try to squeeze through here," she said, and, before Ranger Bill could say anything, she'd disappeared. Koko could see Ranger Bill didn't want to go, but after a minute he elbowed his way after Michelle.

As soon as the humans vanished, Koko scrambled into the front seat and stood at attention, staring at the spot where they'd disappeared. Very shortly the leaves and grasses moved. Koko yelped in surprise at the group who issued forth: first, bedraggled Rosa, her spaniel eyes rimmed with red; next, Ranger Bill carrying a weary wet-looking Jenny, and finally, Michelle, Piccolo's sharp little terrier head limp over her arm, his body cradled against hers.

As, one by one, the tired dogs were placed inside the truck, Piccolo roused himself enough to cry, "Koko, we ran too far trying to help. But I knew you'd come to take us home."

When they reached Shoretown, Ranger Bill drove first to the mayor's house, into which he carried Jenny. Next they dropped off little Piccolo. Rosa's humans were still on vacation, so she was invited into Koko's house and offered a seat in the soft armchair that Koko was allowed in only when she was sick (and couldn't enjoy it).

Rosa's chin rested on the edge of the plush seat cushion. Her silky ears dotted with burrs flopped down toward the floor. "This morning, since you weren't here," she low-barked to Koko, "and Handsome and Bowser hadn't come back yet, Jenny and I decided to run north to the shed and see what was going on. Piccolo wanted to come too. Well, we made it there all right, but those two were as slow as turtles compared to you and me, Koko."

"But you got to the shed?"

Rosa continued, "There's good news and bad news. The good news is Handsome, Bowser and the others have escaped."

Her eyelids closed sleepily.

"And the bad news?" Koko barked.

"Koko, don't bother Rosa," Michelle called from the kitchen. "She's exhausted."

"Rosa," the Aussie low-barked. "The bad news? Handsome and Bowser?"

Rosa opened her eyes halfway. "Those two dopes never ran home at all. None of the dogs did."

"They didn't?" Koko asked, her heart sinking.

"No. We followed their trail for a while. It led in the opposite direction from home."

"The opposite direction?" Koko's ears flattened, and she crouched down and looked aside.

"Yes," Rosa growled. "Instead, those fools ran straight into the woods."

Chapter 22

That Friday evening Jenny, Koko and Piccolo lay with their heads on their paws on the grocery store porch, waiting for Handsome and Bowser to come home. Now and then Koko jumped to her feet restlessly. "Where are they?"

"Out chasing deer, I guess," Jenny growled. "Those two just want to have fun."

They watched as cars parked and people went into the town hall. "What are the humans doing?" Koko whined.

"Oh, they go in there and talk a lot and then go home." Jenny sighed and pulled herself up. "My human stands in front of them. Let's go over and watch him."

Obediently, Koko and Piccolo trotted over to sit with their alpha on the sidewalk outside the town hall. Through the wide double doors, the dogs saw the townspeople move into a large room filled with rows of chairs. Certain humans smiled or petted the dogs. Others walked by without looking at them. A few glared.

Koko raised her head to sniff. She had recognized all the townspeople, friendly or not. But now an unfamiliar human was approaching. And yet she recognized the smell. Grass . . . garbage . . . the envelope Michelle had picked up from Mrs. Gates' lawn . . .

"Jenny," Koko high-barked, "that one." Koko pointed her muzzle toward a gray-haired stranger who was walking toward the hall with the mayor. "She's bad too."

The woman stopped in front of the dogs. "Now here's a perfect example," she said to Jenny's human. "These dogs out here on their own at night, barking like that. Why, anything might happen to them."

"Yes, yes. Well, perhaps you have a point," the mayor murmured, with a friendly wink at Jenny. He was a tall sloppily dressed man with a fringe of long brown hair around his bald head. "Now let me introduce you to . . ." and they moved on.

Koko stood erect, her fur on end, and stared hard at the woman's back, then looked among the humans for Michelle. "Koko, I'm here," Michelle called, waving from a seat in the front row where she sat next to Ranger Bill. "Stay outside, honey. STAY. STAY." Her words carried through the hubbub of human voices that filled the hall.

Koko curled her lip and raised her hackles as she leaned forward stiff-legged staring at the gray-haired woman's back.

But all Michelle did was yell STAY a few more times.

Koko sighed, closed her lips and drew back.

"Good dog," Michelle called.

After a while everyone sat down except the mayor who made a short speech that included the word *Nightingale*. Everyone started clapping. The gray-haired woman climbed up the two steps to the podium and began to speak.

Koko could tell at once that the woman was casting some sort of spell over the humans. They quieted, just as if they'd all been given shots at the vet. The woman's voice was clear and mesmerizing. She extended her arms as if asking for the other humans' help. Her eyes filled with unspilled tears. Love and concern poured out of her.

"Why are they listening to her?" Koko whimpered to Jenny.

"They're ashamed," Jenny growled.

"What's *ashamed*?" Piccolo asked.

"Like when you chased the wrong man."

The woman drew out a large picture of a small bird flying through the air, looking tired but resolute. "Imagine being this bird."

The audience stirred and leaned forward. Koko saw that even Michelle seemed captivated.

"You have just completed a grueling flight of thousands of miles from your nesting grounds in Peru and you're headed for your winter quarters in Northern California. You've flown day and night, with nothing to eat or drink in the four days it's taken you to make the trip. You fly unerringly to the spot your ancestors have flown to for generations, you look down for the green field and blue pond that are your destination . . . "

The woman paused. Koko could sense the expectation in the room.

"And they're gone."

There were sighs and murmurs of dismay.

"All you see are the roofs of condos, the shiny tops of cars, the gray strips of pavement. No green field, no pond.

"You're exhausted. You've already flown more than twice as far as seems possible, given the minute amount of food you ate before you took off.

"From deep in yourself you summon the energy to keep flying. You beat your small wings, you scan the earth below, all rooftop and car and pavement. On you fly. Nothing guides you now. The place your ancestors have landed since birds first flew over this continent has vanished.

"Another hour passes. Your vision is blurred from lack of food and sleep, but you make out a vast body of blue water in the distance, then a yellow strip of sand. It is not the green field or the pond, but there are no cars or roofs there.

"You fly lower from exhaustion. You keep beating your little wings. You're almost there. The yellow sand is dotted with bits of brown. Perhaps there will be some seeds. Perhaps the water will refresh you.

"Finally, you alight. You want to crumple, but you force yourself to peck at a little wet seaweed for nourishment. Yes, this can sustain you. You glance inland

and see green grasses. Yes, if you can make it to the grasses, you can build a nest and . . .

"You see it coming, a huge dark thing, its mouth open, its feet racing. A day ago you might have been able to lift yourself up into the air away from it, and you try now. You reach deep into yourself. You try to fly. You try . . . you try . . .

"But you don't have the strength. You feel the dog's confusion for he expected you to fly up so he could chase you. In the next second his running rear foot flings you into the air, and you feel a great pain in your chest. When you land the dog has moved far down the beach. He may pass you again. Maybe he'll sniff you on his way back, but you'll hardly notice, just flutter a wing in fear. And the next day when he bounds up again you won't move at all, for by then you will have died of starvation."

The woman stopped speaking, and for a moment there was silence. Koko could sense the humans' upset.

Then the woman continued, "This has been an emotional appeal, but now let me give you the facts.

"The Golden Gate National Recreation Area did a study to try to find out how we could save the snowy plover. They found that a snowy plover nesting in the grasses may hop a few steps if a human jogger or walker comes within twelve feet. But an unleashed dog running by at that distance will cause the bird to fly into the air. How can these little birds lay and hatch their eggs if a dog may at any moment appear?

"I know Shoretown has always been a champion of individual freedom and that many of you want your dogs to have that same freedom. You enjoy the sight, you love the thought, of your dog racing full out after some gull, having the time of his or her life. But, unfortunately, the days have passed when we can safely ignore the impact of our enjoyments on Mother Earth.

"Tonight, when you people vote on the proposed leash law for Shoretown, I hope you'll remember everything I've said. Please take the higher road, the wiser course. Your dogs have you watching over them, feeding, sheltering and loving them." She held up her picture again. "This little bird had no one."

Koko was confused. Yes, the woman had something to do with the plot against the dogs, but the love and sympathy Koko sensed in her were real. As the mayor escorted her out, Koko felt two urges: to bite the woman's stockinged leg, and to lick her worried face.

"She's a *Nightingale*," Koko said to Jenny and Piccolo, as they watched the woman get into a long low car and drive away.

"What's that mean?"

"I thought it meant *bad human*. But now I don't know."

The mayor squatted to tousle the dogs' heads and then hurried back into the town hall and its babble of voices.

"Hear, hear, Michelle has the floor next," he called. "Everybody will have his or her five minutes to speak, but one at a time, please."

There were grumbles, but the room grew quieter as Michelle moved to the podium.

"That was a very moving speech," Michelle began. Koko felt better, hearing Michelle's clear voice. She gazed admiringly at her human who was wearing a gray and red turtleneck, her hair in a tail down her back. "And not easy to respond to. Of course we don't want our dogs ruining the lives of courageous little birds nor contributing to the extinction of species. But we don't have the right to just lock them up. Our dogs have their own community here in Shoretown. We're all used to seeing them saying hello to each other in the street or lying together on the road or trotting purposefully on their business. Free dogs are part of Shoretown. It wouldn't be the same here without them. They're part of why we choose to live here.

"Sure, our dogs are sometimes exasperating and do things we don't approve of, but so do most of our family members and friends, and we don't have them locked up."

People chuckled.

"It was dogs that tore apart my sheep last night," Russ Harding said bluntly, and the laugh died.

"Let Michelle have her say, Russ," the mayor put in.

"There've been other things lately besides the sheep-killing," Michelle said. "Things that seem to incriminate our dogs. Every day we witness some new offense. It wouldn't be crazy to deduce that there's a pack of wild dogs on the loose terrorizing our town."

There was a swell of confirming voices.

"Even though," Michelle's voice rose, "no one has caught a glimpse of these wild dogs or seen incriminating tracks or scat. All we've seen are collars, tags, bits of fur—evidence a human being could easily arrange."

Again, people's voices rose, this time in protest.

"I know. A few days ago, I wouldn't have believed it either," Michelle said, "but Koko found a bullet in Russ's dead sheep."

The word *bullet* ricocheted around the room.

"I don't want to speculate further at this point. But Bill and I have been gathering evidence. What I want you all to consider is delaying this leash law vote until we know the whole story."

In a moment Michelle sat down, and Russ Harding took her place at the podium. "Today I found myself thinking about selling out, folks. Oh, it's not just that dead sheep. There's a nice piece of land near my brother's spread just come up for sale. Shoretown's been good to us, but we've had our problems . . .

"Sure, lots of you love your dogs, but just the cost of maintaining the fences against them is hard on us. Dogs barking at the horses, scaring the sheep—I'd say if this town wants a sheep ranch it needs a leash law.

"Now, this idea of Michelle's that humans are conspiring against our dogs: I find that pretty far-fetched. When your plants start dying and holes appear in your garden, you know you've got a gopher problem. When bird nests are desecrated and garbage spilled and a sheep killed, you know you've got a dog problem.

"And another thing. That speech of Mrs. Nightingale's got to me—got to us all. I think she's right. We've gotten too indulgent with our dogs.

"From my point of view, this leash law is long overdue," he concluded.

On and on the people talked, first one at a time, then several at once. Jenny and Piccolo were asleep on either side of Koko when Ranger Bill finally stood up.

"You all know me," he began. "I'm not particularly soft on dogs, except maybe Koko back there."

At the sound of her name, Koko stood up and stared at him, mouth open, tongue hanging to the side.

"Maybe it's time for Shoretown to have a leash law—I'm not sure. Dogs going missing, sheep killed, birds killed, garbage cans knocked over—none of us want that. But Michelle's right, something fishy's going on. Things may not be as they appear.

"I'd like another week or so to investigate further."

Koko could see that Ranger Bill was alpha to many in the room, but Russ Harding's strong-voiced wife spoke angrily. "This leash law vote has been delayed five months for one reason or another. I'm sick of delay."

There was a rumble of confirmation.

"I need more time," Ranger Bill insisted.

A man called out, "How about half a day? Tomorrow's Saturday. We could meet again at noon."

"Only half a day. I don't know." Ranger Bill frowned.

"Or we vote now," a woman threatened.

Ranger Bill glanced at Michelle. "All right. Noon tomorrow."

As the humans streamed out of the town hall, and Piccolo trotted off with his humans, Koko told Jenny, "I'll sneak out tonight and try to round up Handsome and Bowser."

Jenny stretched her neck and legs, and yawned. "Aren't you tired, Koko? Those two will get fed up living in the woods and come back soon enough."

Koko felt uneasy. "I just can't stand waiting."

Michelle appeared out of the town hall and crouched to hug each of the dogs. "You sweethearts, sitting out here so good like this. I hope we can save Shoretown for you." She pressed them each against her. Koko could feel her human's concern and taste salt tears on her cheek. She struggled to lick all of Michelle's face.

"Come on, Koko, say goodnight to Jenny and Piccolo, and let's go home and get a good night's sleep," Michelle said finally, standing up.

"I swear I'll get those dogs back," Koko low-barked to Jenny after she'd licked the alpha's mouth goodnight.

Later, after Michelle and Ranger Bill had fallen asleep, Koko padded to her dog door. Her humans wouldn't wake up until morning. She had until then to run to the shed, pick up the dogs' trail into the woods, find them, and herd Handsome and Bowser back home.

But she was stopped short. Ranger Bill had closed and locked her dog door. She was trapped for the night.

Chapter 23

Koko slept restlessly. Once she woke with a sense of urgency, ran to her dog door, and banged her head against it with a loud thunk.

Another time, waking whimpering from a dream where Ranger Bill had tied her with five ropes to five trees, Koko went to the bedroom door and stood with her nose almost touching it. She barked loudly: "Either let me out, or drive me back to the bad man's shed immediately."

For a moment nothing happened. Then Michelle cracked open the bedroom door and tiptoed out. "For goodness' sake, be quiet, Koko. We're trying to sleep."

Koko ran into the kitchen and over to her closed dog door. She stood before it.

"Go on out, then," Michelle whispered, from the doorway.

Koko butted her head against it.

"What, is something wrong?" Michelle padded over the linoleum in her bare feet. "Oh, he's locked it." She started to unlatch it, then stopped. "But you did your business on the way back from the meeting, Koko. You want to run off somewhere, don't you? No, I'm not letting you out." She snapped the latch back on. "Now, go to sleep." She looked at her watch. "We'll be getting up in a few hours, and I want you here."

Whimpering with disappointment, Koko trudged back to her place under the coffee table.

At last the sky outside lightened a little. Koko sat eagerly beside the bedroom door, waiting for Michelle to hurry and get up. It wasn't long before she came shuffling out in her slippers, murmured hello to Koko, patted her head, and disappeared in the bathroom. A few minutes later, Michelle came out of the bathroom and hurried into the kitchen. Koko followed. Another short time passed and Michelle carried two cups of something hot out of the kitchen and into the bedroom, leaving the door open so Koko could follow her in, jump on the bed and curl up between Ranger Bill, who was murmuring sleepily, and Michelle, who was sipping her tea and saying, "Careful, Koko."

As Ranger Bill came awake and struggled up against the headboard to drink his coffee, Koko rolled over on her back and waved her four feet in the air so he could pet her stomach. She lay in a daze, listening to the two humans sipping their drinks, smelling the coffee's sharp aroma mixed with their body smells, Michelle's salty and spicy and Ranger Bill's deeper and more pungent.

"Isn't she the cutest dog?" Michelle murmured, and Ranger Bill agreed.

Then Koko remembered that Handsome and Bowser might be home by now. She struggled to her feet, knocking Ranger Bill's arm so he spilled hot coffee on the bedclothes. As the Aussie jumped off the bed to run to the kitchen, Michelle called after her, "For heaven's sakes."

As soon as Michelle came into the kitchen, Koko rushed to her dog door to be let out. But Michelle hesitated, saying, "We want you with us this morning, honey," and, getting a leash out of the hall closet, clipped it to Koko's collar. Koko was forced to pee in the back yard with Michelle watching and then follow Michelle back into the closed house.

As sunlight hit the tops of the trees, Ranger Bill helped Koko and Michelle into his truck, then drove out to the highway and headed north. When he turned up the curvy road toward the shed, Koko leaned forward, her paws on the back of the seat. The gate was open, and they continued up a winding drive to a big stone house. The woman who'd made the speech the night before came smiling to greet them.

When she saw her, Koko bared her teeth and growled.

"Koko, quiet. I know you don't like that poor woman, but can't you behave?" Michelle said. "Now, STAY."

She opened the truck door, and one hand on Koko's collar, got out and closed the door in the Aussie's face. Koko sat staring out the window, sensing that, even though the three humans were smiling at each other and talking pleasantly, underneath their hackles were raised.

"Actually, even having a dog on the grounds is hard on the birds," the gray-haired woman said.

"Yes, so sorry," Michelle said. "What a nice place you have here," she went on. "I've been hearing about this place for years, but haven't had a chance to visit until now."

"Can we take a look around?" Ranger Bill asked.

"Certainly. Let me show you some of my most recent discoveries," Mrs. Nightingale answered. "It's good you came so early. The birds will still be singing." And, putting her arms through theirs, she led them down a path away from the house and into the woods.

"That's not the direction of the shed," Koko barked. "It's not that way."

But Michelle just turned and yelled, "Quiet, Koko."

Koko watched them vanish. Maybe they'd circle around. She sat trying to be patient.

Familiar smells wafted through the cracked-open windows.

The oily smell of the van—that old gray vehicle parked nearby.

The strong fishy feathery smell on the breeze—the falcon who had killed the snowy plover at Seal Beach.

The flowery smell—the woman who had just steered Michelle and Ranger Bill off in the wrong direction.

And most infuriating—the smell of the man, all metallic and smoky and bitter.

Outraged, Koko began to scratch angrily at the opening Michelle had left at the top of the window.

After a few minutes, she gave up and sat back in resignation. What was the use? She was a prisoner. Dogs were constantly being locked up. She must just wait. It was getting warmer closed up in here, and she better not over-exert herself.

Koko slumped back in the passenger seat.

After what seemed a long time she smelled Michelle and Ranger Bill returning with the flowery-smelling woman. Koko sat up and watched. Michelle looked thoughtful as she walked a little behind the other two who appeared deep in conversation. The three humans were heading toward the truck.

"We appreciate your showing us so much of the place," Ranger Bill said. "Of course, it's too vast to see everything."

"Four thousand acres and most of it still untouched by human hand," Mrs. Nightingale said. "Just as my father left it."

"By the way," Ranger Bill said. "I understand your son Andrew is back living with you. He went to high school with my younger brother, you know."

It seemed to Koko that a shadow crossed Mrs. Nightingale's face, but she said brightly, "Andrew, yes, he should be around. That's his van there.

"Andrew?" she called toward the house, and, when there was no answer, "Gone off on one of his walks, I expect. He loves birds too, you know. I'll tell him you asked after him."

Koko stared hard through the window at Michelle's face as she came up to the passenger door. Their eyes met, and it seemed to Koko a current passed between them. Michelle opened the truck door, commanding, "Stay, Koko."

But sensing the encouragement of her human, who continued to hold the door open, Koko leapt down to the gravel and raced off in the direction of the shed.

"Koko, come back," Michelle cried.

"Stop your dog," Mrs. Nightingale screamed.

"Koko," Ranger Bill roared.

For a moment the force of his yell slowed Koko. But no, she must disobey. She sped on past the house, the humans after her, and down a narrow path toward the fresh watery odor of the waterfall and the mawna smell of the shed.

At one point, she glanced back at Michelle who was shouting without conviction, "Koko, stay. Koko, come back."

On Koko ran, not so slowly that the humans could catch her and not so fast that they would give up following her. She heard the roar of the waterfall and spotted the tumbling creek, the wooden bridge and the shed.

The gate to the yard was open, and the door to the shed was open too. Koko heard a loud crack, as if a human had kicked a wall. As Michelle, Ranger Bill and Mrs. Nightingale came puffing across the bridge, a man stomped out of the shed, yelling, "Damn." He heaved a black case down on the ground, where it flew open, spilling wires and metal clips.

Nearby, Koko spied a handsome brown bird with yellow on its face and a curved beak settle itself on a branch as it watched the humans with cool eyes.

Koko trotted around to the back of the shed and hurriedly sniffed the bank of the river. She could hear Ranger Bill and Michelle's aggressive questions and the defensive answers of the woman and man.

Racing back around the shed, the Aussie streaked past the four humans and over the bridge, hot on the trail of the lost dogs. Behind her, Michelle's commands rang out, grew fainter, disappeared.

Koko was on a narrow animal path—here and there she saw a flicker of deer fur or a wisp of dog hair caught on a twig or a spear of grass. Once, spotting a squirrel nibbling at an acorn between its paws, she dashed over to chase it up a tree. But as she eyed it chattering down at her, she remembered her duty and resumed tracking, settling into a swift even pace as the dogs' scents led farther into the woods.

Suddenly she heard a commotion of dogs barking and twigs breaking. In a moment Bowser appeared, his fur tangled and dirty, his paws bloody. He crossed the path ahead, racing as if his life depended on it. A few feet behind him, barking viciously, raced a thin-looking Handsome, followed by a big brown and black dog and two hounds. Before Koko could act, Handsome had grabbed Bowser's back leg, Bowser had crashed down with a yelp, and the dogs had surrounded him with such growling and slavering that Koko was sure they were about to tear the puppy apart and eat him.

Chapter 24

Koko growled and curled her lip at the bigger dogs, who had clearly gone loco.

"Koko, what are you doing here?" Bowser yipped from his place on the ground, his throat bared beneath Handsome's teeth.

Handsome looked up, tail wagging. "Koko, you've come to join us."

Koko's ears flattened as she eyed the dogs uneasily.

"We're practicing hunting in a pack," Bowser barked. "I'm the rabbit."

"I'm so glad you came." Handsome's tail waved broadly as he licked Koko's mouth in greeting and then introduced her to Toro and the hounds. The dogs were all thin and excited and smelled of the woods.

"Why didn't you come home?"

"Are they missing us at home?" Handsome's otter tail went between his legs.

"Of course they are," Koko barked.

Bowser jumped to his feet. "But Koko, we can't go home. We've gone wild."

Koko closed her mouth and stared at him.

"Just like the Wild Bunch. Haven't we, Toro?"

"That's right. And you . . ." The big dog moved to rest his chin on Koko's shoulder, impressing his leadership on her. "Don't try to tame us again. Now," he turned away from her, "some of us have to get ready for our war party. Let's get back to camp. "

Koko studied her two friends as they trotted after Toro and the others. Handsome and Bowser were excited in a way she didn't remember. "Do you like it here so much you don't want to go back to Shoretown?"

"We want to go back," Handsome barked, "but . . . "

Bowser yipped eagerly, "Tell her about our hunts."

"We went on a hunt yesterday and almost brought down a deer. Then this morning we almost brought down a rabbit."

"'Almost?'" Koko barked. "Aren't you hungry?"

"Very hungry. But Toro says that's how it is in the wild." Bowser looked up as an animal scurried in the branches above. "Last night we found a dead rabbit, but we had to split it—all I got was some fur and a bone the size of my claw."

As they came out into an opening in the trees a large golden retriever raised her head from where she was resting under the shade of a bay tree with two other dogs.

"Goldie, it's Koko," Bowser barked, running over to her.

The golden retriever stood and, walking gracefully over, her dirty tail waving, she sniffed Koko politely.

Koko barked impatiently, "Everyone's waiting for you dogs at home."

Goldie's mild yellow eyes hardened. "Our humans have a leash law in Porcupine City. When we get home they'll just tie us up. They can live without us for a few days more."

Leash law. The husky in Porcupine City had been bitter when he'd used those words too. Koko was glad Shoretown didn't have a *leash law*.

"Goldie and Toro have arranged the entire camp," Bowser told Koko eagerly. "That flat place under the tree is where we nap, and that dense brush is where we'll hide in case of an attack. Once we've caught some food we'll . . . well, we have a cave picked out to bury it in. And that path goes down to the water, but the mangy old coyote who's in the cave won't let us pass."

"A coyote!" Koko had seen coyotes occasionally, usually at night, but they'd always disappeared before she could get close. You usually saw only one coyote at a time—they rarely traveled in packs like dogs. They had a powerful unsettling smell and communicated by screaming.

Bowser went on, "Toro's organized a war party starting in a few minutes. You can come too, Koko. We're going to seize that cave for our own. You should see that old coyote. He's small and beat-up and mean looking. Toro says, if the Wild Bunch needed that cave to store their game, they'd just take it. So that's what we're going to do."

"But you haven't caught any game," Koko barked.

Goldie added, "That coyote has a mate and pups in that cave he's guarding."

"So what?" said Bowser. "He can move them somewhere else."

Just then Toro sounded a sharp bark, and dogs bounded to join him. After a short huddle, the five members of the war party, barking ferociously, raced down the short path that led to the creek.

Almost immediately there was a sharp yelp and then silence.

Koko and Goldie trotted around a boulder to see the five dogs crouched low to the ground in a semi-circle, looking up at a scrawny gray coyote. The coyote sat on a ledge blocking the entrance to a small cave. It seemed he was alpha, even for Toro.

The coyote spoke in a complaining voice that was impossible to ignore. "You dogs are scaring all the game away from these parts. How long do you plan to be fooling around here?"

"Forever," Bowser burst out. "We're wild dogs now."

"We're hunters," Handsome barked. "We tire the game out one day so we can catch it the next. This morning we almost caught a rabbit."

"Anyway, who do you think you are, King of the Forest?" Toro barked.

The coyote's sharp eyes glided over Toro and rested on Handsome. "How close did you come to that rabbit?"

"One more pounce, and I would have had it."

"A rabbit will let you get that close. It doesn't mean anything. If you'd been able to put on speed, the rabbit would have too. Unless it was sick."

"That's not true," Handsome protested. "I once caught a rabbit. And it was a healthy rabbit and tasted good too."

Armed with more confidence, the dogs shifted a little closer to the coyote, growling and baring their teeth.

"Those fools," Goldie low-barked to Koko. "Going up against a coyote."

"So, you caught a healthy rabbit," the coyote said. "My, that is impressive. Perhaps, if you lived here in the woods, you could catch another one every day. That is, at least one, for your friends here may not be as quick as you, and they'd need food too."

"Sure I could," Handsome barked, but Koko saw his ears had flattened in doubt.

"In this cave," the coyote said, "are my mate and our five pups. We don't want you dogs around. Can't you play at being wild somewhere else?"

"This camp is perfect for us," Toro barked. "We need that cave to store our provisions. Now get out and make it snappy." With this Toro suddenly rushed forward, there was a loud scuffle, and Toro slunk back and sat down, blood dripping down his forehead into his eye. The coyote once more sat surveying the dogs.

Goldie rolled on her back, waving her paws in the air. "I apologize on behalf of my friend. I am a friendly female. May I approach your mate and see your little ones?"

The coyote stared at her for a moment and then shifted to the side. "Be my guest."

Goldie's sweeping tail disappeared into the darkness of the cave, there was a sharp yelp, and she came scrambling back out.

The coyote said, "No coyote mother is going to let a stranger in with her pups. She won't even let me in."

Goldie sat down in the semicircle of dogs looking up at the coyote, and raised a paw in deference.

"This is just another example of how you dogs know nothing of life in the wild," the coyote harangued them in his annoying voice. "I can see you need some enlightenment. For instance, do you know of those five pups in there, only one will survive past ten months?"

"Only one?" Bowser yipped in shock, wondering if his litter-mates, with whom he'd tumbled, were dead too.

"One will be shot, one will be poisoned, one will be caught in a trap and left to die and another will die of distemper. If anything happens to me at this point, if I break a leg or hurt my back so I can't run, they all may die.

"Life in the wild is constant worry. Every time I take a nap I have to be half-awake and ready to fight in case another coyote tries to take over my territory. Any dead animal I find I have to examine with care, no matter how tired or hungry I am. Otherwise I may be carrying home poisoned meat to my family. Every time I smell a human I have to hide. My life is spent sneaking around and running away." The coyote's voice had an anguished, self-pitying tone.

"But aren't you happy, being free?" Koko asked.

"Free? What am I free of? I can't go where I want, eat what I want, rest when I want." The coyote shook his head in disgust.

"But you can run through the woods in the moonlight," Bowser said.

"You can drink from clear springs over gray rocks," Toro added.

"You can bring down game, you can howl at the moon, you can choose your own destiny," Goldie put in.

"You don't have to stay fenced in some yard or be leashed to a human."

"If only some human would want me," the coyote said in a sad low voice different from his normal one.

The dogs glanced at each other in confusion.

"But," the coyote said, resuming his aggrieved tone, "humans hate me."

"But say a human did want you," Koko barked. "You wouldn't mind being leashed or kept at home in a fenced yard? Wouldn't you hate it?"

The coyote considered. "Yes, to be honest, I probably would hate it—"

"You see?" the dogs barked to each other excitedly. "Of course he would hate it."

"Let me finish," came the coyote's penetrating voice. "I would hate it at first. But answer me a few questions. Would I be fed and given fresh water every day?"

"Oh, yes. And hamburger," Bowser yipped, drooling.

"Could I lie down and nap without fear of anyone pouncing on me?"

"The only thing that might happen is your human might come to take you for a walk."

"Or to the vet," Handsome put in.

The coyote asked what a *vet* was, and when he heard the answer, shook his head. "Your humans take you to be healed when you're sick?" This seemed to touch him. His thin pointed mouth opened and closed a few times. "It's like *The Loved Ones*," he finally said. "I never believed that myth, but now I wonder."

"*The Loved Ones*?" Goldie asked.

"Oh, just a silly sentimental myth," the coyote said dismissingly. "I shouldn't have mentioned it. I don't know what came over me."

"Tell us," Koko barked.

"No, there's no point."

All the dogs begged him to tell them.

The coyote demurred for another few minutes and finally gave in. "Once there were two young coyotes, little females, who were orphaned, their mother and father both shot by a rancher. Two humans, different from the rest, adopted the two little sisters and they lived with those humans all their lives. *The Loved Ones* could nap whenever they liked. They could play in a big dusty yard, and they were given food and fresh water in their own special dishes every day. When they were sick or had thorns in their paws, the humans healed them. When they were old, the humans took extra care of them. When they were ready to pass over, the humans helped. As a pup, every coyote hears about *The Loved Ones*. Every coyote parent hopes that if anything happens to them, their pups might be as fortunate as *The Loved Ones*." The coyote's voice had become tremulous, and now he seemed to shrink before their eyes as he let his fur stand down.

The dogs were silent for a moment, and Koko could feel a wave of nostalgia as thick as gravy roll over them.

"Do they really miss us back home?" Handsome whimpered to Koko.

"Terribly."

The coyote's ear twitched, but otherwise he appeared sunken in sadness.

Toro stood up and shook himself. "*Loved Ones* or not," he growled, "don't think that means we're just going to high-tail it out of here, leaving you a clear field."

Although Toro spoke with confidence, Koko noticed that the other dogs did not join in, but remained wistful.

"I want to go home," Bowser yelped suddenly.

"Be a dog, Bowser," Toro snapped.

Koko barked, "Bowser, Handsome, there's lots of food waiting at home. Hamburger, liver treats, chicken . . . Plus your humans will be so glad to see you."

Handsome whined, "I miss my humans, but I want to be a wild dog."

"Of course you do," Toro urged.

"I've been a wild dog long enough," Bowser said. "I've eaten fur and hunted food and slept out all night. Come on, Handsome, don't you want to go home with Koko?"

"Dog-gone-it, I do." Handsome looked around at the others. "But we've hardly got started here. How can you say you've been a wild dog, Bowser? You haven't done anything really wild."

"Didn't I chase a deer in a pack? Didn't I tear apart a dead rabbit? Don't I have fleas and sores? Didn't I lie under the stars and drink from wild streams? What else should I do? Get scrawny and beat-up like this coyote here?—My apologies," Bowser said to the coyote—"Lie awake half-terrified every night? Get sick and die a long painful death stuck in a bush?"

The annoying voice of the coyote added, "Why don't you two run back to Shoretown as your friend suggests? You can always come back."

"That's true." Handsome's tail waved broadly. "That's true, isn't it, Koko? We can come back." He pranced excitedly. "Yes, let's go home."

As he and Bowser exchanged goodbyes with the other dogs, Koko low-barked to the coyote, "Your story of *The Loved Ones* was very moving."

"It's true I have a creative gift," the coyote agreed. "And there's a grain of truth to it."

Chapter 25

Jenny stood, her nose pressed against a wire mesh fence. Behind it a white dog stood in a large yard. A few yards away a car zoomed by on the highway, trailing exhaust.

Jenny was worried. Piccolo had told her that a big box smelling of new leashes had just been carried from the hardware store to the town hall. "Now, Snowflake, if you smell, see or hear any of these three dogs: Handsome, Bowser or Koko, I want you to howl as loud as you can."

"I'm familiar with Handsome, but the other two I haven't the faintest idea of," the Samoyed said.

Jenny described the dogs. "You howl, and Rex down the road will pick it up and pass it on."

Snowflake rolled on her back. "Okay, I'm normally not a howler. But for you, Jenny, I'll do it."

"Good. Your house is so close to the highway, you have to stay locked up. But for the rest of us it may make a world of difference. All the dogs of Shoretown will be grateful to you, and bring you bones."

Jenny trotted back into town. She had no idea where Koko was, but she assumed the Aussie was on the job, trying to find the others. In Jenny's experience, missing dogs brought sweating paws and raised hackles to humans.

Enough to make them angrily open that box of leashes and leash them all.

She stopped for a drink at the muddy puddle in back of the gas station and then lay down on the sidewalk. Five dogs who lived along the route from the highway were set to howl to each other as soon as they saw the missing dogs. There was nothing more to be done, but keep an eye on the door behind which sat the box of new leashes.

The sun was overhead when the door suddenly opened. Jenny sat up worriedly. She watched as the same cars that had appeared the night before showed up, and the same people climbed out of them and entered the town hall.

Ranger Bill arrived, not with Michelle, but with two other people: the gray-haired woman who'd enraptured the crowd the night before and Russ Harding, the rancher who'd owned the sheep that was killed.

Jenny studied these two. Unlike last night, when the gray-haired woman had smelled assured and powerful, she now seemed frightened. Her eyes were red-rimmed, as if she'd been weeping, and when she turned to Ranger Bill and the rancher she spoke, not like the alpha she'd been last night, but like a dog wanting a favor. The burly rancher was excited—his eyes were bright, and he smelled of sweat.

In a few minutes Jenny's human, the mayor, quieted the people down. The room rustled with sandwiches being unwrapped. Soda cans were snapped open. Jenny estimated there must have been at least three of the grocery store's roast beef sandwiches. They were the mayor's favorite, and, whenever he ate one, he always pulled out a chunk of beef and tossed it to her.

"We'll start with Bill's report. He's got some new information for us," the mayor said.

Ranger Bill stood up. All he said was, "Mrs. Nightingale has something important to say to you all."

The gray-haired woman moved to the front of the room and began in a trembling voice that slowly grew firmer. "Last night, in speaking to you, I spoke truthfully—I did believe a leash law was the right direction for

Shoretown—but today I must eat humble pie. My son Andrew, whom some of you know, has been living with me for the past month or so—he left abruptly a few hours ago, or he'd be with me now, standing before you.

"I must make heartfelt apologies to you. I'm afraid Andrew was responsible for two of your dogs going missing—Handsome and Bowser, I believe their names were."

There was a moment of stunned silence and then, "Are they all right?" came a woman's tight voice.

"I'm sure they're all right," Mrs. Nightingale reassured her.

"As far as we know," Ranger Bill added, half-rising, "the dogs are unharmed and loose in the woods at the moment. They're probably on their way home now. Michelle's putting up signs on the highway warning drivers to be on the lookout for them."

"The highway," Daisy, Bowser's human, cried. "They're near the highway? What woods do you mean? Is it the Nightingale Bird Sanctuary? That means they'll have to cross the highway to come home. Can't you put up a road block?"

"I don't think we'd be able to arrange that," Ranger Bill answered. "These are savvy dogs and, as I said, Michelle is putting up signs warning cars to drive slowly."

"As if anyone's going to pay attention," Handsome's male human scoffed. "We should all be out looking for them, not sitting here listening to her."

"Mrs. Nightingale has something important to say," Ranger Bill said. "Take a few minutes to listen. Remember, it's vital you all stay for the leash law vote."

"Who cares about the vote? Bowser may be getting run over this very minute," Daisy cried. Jenny saw her squeeze past the others in her row and bolt out of the meeting, hardly glancing at Jenny as she ran to her car.

Ranger Bill motioned for the gray-haired woman to proceed.

"Andrew was trying to retrain the dogs not to chase birds. He only took a dog if he actually caught it in the act of chasing a bird, you see. The retraining was to take only a few hours—at least, that's what he told me. Of course I was very remiss. I should have put my foot down right away, but I was so pleased to have him home . . . "

Mrs. Nightingale shook her head. "It was Andrew who made it look as if a dog attacked the snowy plover nest at Seal Beach. It was Andrew who made it look as if a dog spilled the garbage at the Gates' estate. It was Andrew who shot one of Mr. Harding's sheep and made it appear a pack of dogs had killed it."

There was a restless murmur in the room. Jenny could feel that, at the same time the humans were angry, many of them sympathized with the gray-haired woman. The alpha's hackles rose, and she growled low.

"Andrew had caught ten dogs by the time they dug a hole in the shed floor and escaped into the woods—"

"Shame on you," someone called.

"And to think you were taking the high road last night," someone else cried, and the room filled with voices.

"If the dogs don't show up soon, the Park Service will mount a thorough search," Ranger Bill said loudly, looking toward the door where Jenny sat.

"In reparation and in hopes that you will forgive me and my son Andrew," Mrs. Nightingale raised her voice over the hubbub, "I am making a gift to the town of the Harding Ranch."

As the woman's words registered, people stopped talking.

"Russ Harding has generously agreed to sell it to me—"

The middle-aged rancher stood up, hoisting his jeans. His gravelly voice filled the hall. "Yeah, I've decided to get out and buy that place up north near my brother's spread. Mrs. Nightingale made me an offer I couldn't refuse."

Mrs. Nightingale continued, "My lawyer is drawing up the papers as we speak. The fields, the woods, the three gullies, the strip of beach known as Hidden Beach—about five hundred acres in all—is to be used in perpetuity," she cleared her throat, "by dogs."

Chapter 26

"Dogs?" someone echoed.

"Yes," the gray-haired woman said. "The conditions of the gift—and I should mention that your fellow townswoman Michelle was instrumental in spelling these conditions out—require that no dog ever be refused entrance to the land by gate or human, that the land be free from development in perpetuity, that no structures be built on it, nor farm animals grazed there, nor crops grown there. In other words, this is to be dog, not human, land. My own hope is that having a place of their own will keep the dogs from disturbing wildlife in other areas. A further condition is that the path currently used by the dogs to get to the snowy plover nesting site on Seal Beach be immediately blocked and that the beach eventually be fenced."

"What about your house and farm buildings, Russ?" a woman asked.

The rancher answered, "Part of the package."

"They will be sold separately, the proceeds invested, and the interest used to pay taxes and other fees for the dogs' land," Mrs. Nightingale said.

Jenny sensed the growing excitement in the room.

"What a waste of prime oceanfront land," one man said. "How could you be party to this, Russ? Dogs, of all things."

The sheep rancher answered, "Tell you the truth, it's all happened so quickly I haven't had much time to think about it. It's a crazy idea, I'll grant you that, giving a big chunk of land like that to dogs. But at least they're not going to be building condos on it, like the last guy to make me an offer. The pooches will make paths and dig holes and keep the rabbits and squirrels on their toes—that's about the extent of it, I figure. Shoretown could do worse."

"Much worse," someone called out. "Thank you, Russ."

Just then Michelle came breathlessly up to the door, stopped there to scratch Jenny's head, and muttered, "Koko's not here yet. Where is she?" After Michelle had made her way to a seat in the front row beside Ranger Bill, Jenny saw them whisper together, Michelle shaking her head.

"What about the vote on the leash law?" a bearded man called. "I didn't come down here today to join some canine love fest. I don't care how many acres are devoted to dogs as long as they're properly fenced and don't come doing their business in my yard, chasing my cats, knocking over my garbage and sauntering out in front of my car. I want that leash law passed, regardless."

"Hear, hear," someone cried.

Jenny stiffened at the aggression in the air.

"Look, there are three dogs missing from this town right now," the bearded man continued. "Okay, so two of them were stolen rather than lost, but that doesn't change the fact that three families are grieving who wouldn't have had to if the leash law had been in effect a couple of weeks ago. Let's vote this in before more dogs go missing."

Michelle rose in protest. "Koko will be back. You'll see. And Handsome and Bowser too."

"Dogs running around in the wild—well, you just can't predict what they'll do," a woman said. "I agree, let's get on with this vote, Mayor. Seems to me we've delayed long enough."

The mayor stood up, and hoisted his pants. "All right. I was hoping those lost dogs of ours might be back before we voted, but, you're right, people have to get back to their jobs and families—we can't wait all day. Now, let's see, I guess I'd better read you the text of the proposed law again so you'll know what you're voting on." He leafed through some papers in a manila folder on the podium. "Let's see, where is that? These things are never around when you need them."

"Here's a copy, Mayor," the woman who'd just spoken said, hurrying to the front of the room to hand him a folded newspaper, "in today's paper."

"Oh, right, right." The mayor cleared his throat, and slowly read, "'All dogs within the town limits must be fenced or leashed. Violating owners will be fined a hundred dollars.' Okay, then, is everyone clear on that? Anyone suggest any change in that wording?"

Michelle raised her hand. "I think we should reconsider that fine. A hundred dollars seems steep to me."

Someone called out, "We hashed this out months ago and agreed that this is how it's to read. Let's vote on the darned thing. If it's defeated, then we can talk about a different wording for next time."

"Yes, yes. He's right, you know," the mayor said to Michelle. He sighed and squeezed his nose. "All right, let's start with a show of hands. All those in favor of this law that I just read?"

Jenny stood in the doorway, watching uneasily. All the humans who didn't like her and some of those who did were raising their hands, and she didn't know why. The humans had used the word *leash* a lot. Did this have to do with the box of leashes?

"Against?" the mayor asked.

People lowered their hands, and other people raised theirs.

"Too close to call," the mayor said. "We'll need a paper vote."

Jenny watched as the mayor, who had rescued her from the pound, searched through the drawers of a dusty desk at the side of the room, pulling out sheets of paper, shoving them back and searching again. "Anyone have a ruler?" he asked the room at large.

"Dad blast, I'll rip the damned paper," someone said.

"No, no, this must be a proper vote." The mayor folded the paper in quarters, and then spent some time ripping it along the folds.

As he came back to the front of the room, his gaze met Jenny's. She sensed there were tears in his eyes.

As the mayor began handing out the slips of paper, there came a faint howl from far away. And another closer in. And another. Long penetrating howls as if every dog in Shoretown were protesting this unfair law that was about to be passed.

"What's going on?" someone asked.

"I've never heard them do that before," another said.

"The dogs are back," Michelle cried.

Jenny stood staring down Main Street, listening to the chain of howling. She pictured Koko, Handsome and Bowser racing along the lagoon, past the old boat shack, past the horse field. They'd be galloping past the schoolyard, their paws hot on the pavement, their breath coming fast.

She glanced back. The mayor was almost through passing out the ballots.

"So, do we put a 'Yes' if we want the law and a 'No' if we don't?" someone asked.

"I think—" the mayor began and then looked up hopefully as Jenny barked.

Suddenly the humans turned to see three bedraggled dogs sitting side by side in the open doors of the town hall, tongues hanging out, eyes shining.

"Koko," Michelle cried, running down the aisle to embrace her Aussie.

At the same time, Handsome's humans scrambled out of their seats, barged past their neighbors and raced to greet the happy Lab, who jumped up on his hind legs to paw them and lick their faces.

Bowser stood, his stub tail slowly ceasing to wave as he looked around in dismay. "All the other humans are here. Where's mine? Is she still mad at me?"

"Not at all." Jenny licked the top of his head.

"I was in a terrible prison for days and days," he told her. "But I didn't let it get me down. And then I was a member of the Wild Bunch and we hunted food and—"

"Bowser" came a cry from down the street. Bowser whirled and ran straight into the arms of his human.

It took a while for the commotion to die down. One of the men who'd been most impatient for the leash law before brushed a tear from the corner of his eye, stood up and headed for the door.

"Where's your ballot, John?" the mayor called after him.

"Aw, forget it. I don't have time for this," the man said. "Let the people who love them decide about the dogs."

Two other humans nodded in agreement and followed him out.

Jenny stretched her legs and left the hard sidewalk for the soft dirt in back of the town hall. She had learned from the smile on her human's face that the box of leashes was headed back to the hardware store.

In her younger days Jenny had never had time to philosophize, but lately she'd been thinking more, mostly about her ancestors. Millions of years ago they had made the decision that every dog since had had to live with. They had left their wolf packs, become scavengers and finally joined forces with humans.

Had they been right? Today it seemed like maybe they had.

Chapter 27

Seven days after Koko had herded Handsome and Bowser back to Shoretown, a group of dogs were trudging down Pine Street, their tails between their legs.

"So what if they blocked off our path to Seal Beach," Bowser yipped. "I never liked Seal Beach anyway. It's too far."

"Oh, shut up," growled Rosa. "What do you know? That beach has been ours for as long as I remember."

Far down the road by the sheep meadow, a huge truck stood backed up to the gate. Near the truck, a cluster of cars and pick-ups were parked. Sheep were baa-ing, humans were yelling.

The dogs lifted their tails and trotted to investigate.

About twenty brightly colored humans were scattered around the field, trying to persuade thirty cream-colored sheep to funnel into a V-shaped corral, which led into the big truck. Two of the sheep were on the ramp, half a dozen others milled around in the corral, but plenty of young sheep were still out in the meadow dashing about evading the humans.

"They're taking the sheep away," Handsome barked. "Look, aren't there more trucks, way on the other side?"

Far away, across the wide meadow and gullies and hills, Koko spotted three tiny versions of the nearby truck, with white sheep streaming into then.

"I wonder who's moving in." Jenny sat down near the truck to scratch her ear with a hind paw. "Maybe cows will have it. Cows are bigger than sheep."

"Horses are even bigger," Piccolo suggested.

"Whatever animal gets to live there, they're lucky," Handsome barked. "When I was a pup I got to run there once. There's a creek down in that gully and at the end of the gully, a wonderful wild beach that humans never go to.

"And there're squirrels," the Lab continued, waving his otter tail, "and possums and raccoons. And lots of animal holes in the fields."

Koko listened with half an ear. Most of her attention was on the sheep. How she longed to get in there and herd them the proper way. The humans were doing it all wrong. Humans weren't fast enough, and some of them were afraid of the sheep. "Humans," she barked, "Look lively, there. Those sheep are making fools of you."

The sheep heading into the truck started at her bark and tried to turn around.

"Hey. Quiet, you," a man in jeans yelled as he struggled to get the sheep moving properly again.

"Those humans don't have the first idea how to herd sheep," Koko told the other dogs, as she stepped from paw to paw, trembling with eagerness.

"You're an Australian shepherd," Jenny said. "I bet you could herd those sheep."

Although she had never herded sheep in her life, deep inside Koko felt certain the alpha was right. She raced up to the corral, leaped across a fence onto a sheep's woolly back, ran over the backs of other startled sheep, jumped down and streaked across the meadow in pursuit of a runaway.

"Koko," she heard Michelle cry in the distance. "Look at her, Bill."

Koko intercepted the straying sheep, who stopped and drew her head back. The Aussie lowered herself and stared up at the wary eyes in the woolly face. The sheep hesitated, then turned and ran back toward the truck.

Five sheep were disappearing down a path toward the gully. Koko raced through the brush to block them. The lead sheep lowered her head to butt, but, upon seeing Koko eye her, turned suddenly and ran back up the path, the others following.

Returning to the meadow, Koko looked around. Most of the humans had stopped waving their arms and were staring her way. Koko sped toward a scatter of sheep that were frisking in a far corner. The Aussie barked at them to get in line. When they didn't immediately obey, she moved in and snapped at their heels, clicking her teeth together sharply. They jumped back and raced off toward the truck, baa-ing with excitement and alarm.

Now all that was necessary was to keep slowly going back and forth behind the sheep, eyeing any sheep that tried to turn around. Once or twice humans got in the way, but Koko swerved around them, concentrating on her task.

Finally, after all the sheep had been loaded into the truck and driven off, Koko sat panting hard, ears flattened and tongue hanging out. Men packed up the metal corral, and Michelle staggered across the meadow with a sloshing dishpan full of water.

Koko lapped thirstily at the water, then looked up at her friends who, with wagging tails and open mouths, were still outside the half-open gate watching her. The Aussie regarded them with bright happy eyes. She had never felt so like a real dog.

Two humans tinkered with the gate's hinges, while other humans with thick gloves began clipping and rolling up the barbed wire fence.

"Come on, dogs, this land is yours now." Ranger Bill waved the other dogs forward into the meadow.

Koko was puzzled. What was happening was extremely unusual, dogs being invited by Ranger Bill onto farmland. She watched as first Jenny, then Handsome, then the others crept into the meadow, took a sip of water and looked up at Ranger Bill submissively.

"It's yours, Koko," Michelle cried. She said to Bill, "They can't believe it."

Tentatively at first, and then, as Koko and Jenny led them, more swiftly, the dogs ventured out into the meadow.

"I don't know what's going on," Jenny barked to the others as they bounded through the wild grass and low plants, the smells of moles and gophers all around them, "but let's enjoy it while we can. I'm heading for that gully."

"Me too," Piccolo barked.

"Wait, you guys, I'm sure I can catch this mouse." Bowser began furiously digging, scattering dust.

"That creek I smell, wherever it is, is mine." Rosa's silky ears streamed behind her as she ran.

"I'll race you to Hidden Beach," came Handsome's throaty voice at Koko's ear. With a swift glance into his dark eyes, Koko shifted into top speed and together they raced past the others, all else forgotten, headlong into the *Neverendingness*.

Come with Koko on her next adventure

*The savvy Australian Shepherd must discover
why dogs and humans are suddenly revealing
their secret selves in the next*
Koko the Canine Detective Mystery

The Shoretown Dogs Go Loco

www.kokothedetective.com